MOONLIGHT FOR
NURSE CLAIRE

MOONLIGHT FOR NURSE CLAIRE

'I've got more on my mind than Dr Simon Bonham!'

What with passing her finals and helping her hard-up mother and younger brother, Nurse Claire Simms had little time left over for romantic involvements. It was difficult for her to bring herself to admit that she needed the help of the infuriatingly attractive – and interfering – Dr Bonham.

Moonlight For Nurse Claire

by

Sarah Franklin

Dales Large Print Books
Long Preston, North Yorkshire,
BD23 4ND, England.

British Library Cataloguing in Publication Data.

Franklin, Sarah
    Moonlight for Nurse Claire.

    A catalogue record of this book is
    available from the British Library

    ISBN   1-84262-199-8 pbk

First published in Great Britain in 1985 by Mills & Boon Ltd.

Copyright © Sarah Franklin 1985

Cover illustration © Peter Michael by arrangement with
P.W.A. International

The moral right of the author has been asserted

Published in Large Print 2003 by arrangement with
Sarah Franklin, care of Dorian Literary Agency

Dales Large Print is an imprint of Library Magna Books Ltd.

Printed and bound in Great Britain by
T.J. (International) Ltd., Cornwall, PL28 8RW

CHAPTER ONE

The music swelled, assailing Claire's senses like some exotic perfume. Its exquisite vibration almost seemed to lift her feet from the ground. She looked up at the man whose arms encircled her – so tall and handsome in his dark evening dress. He smiled down at her adoringly. The waltz held them in its enchantment and Claire felt as though she were floating – floating on a cloud of rapture. Their steps matched faultlessly as their bodies moved in perfect harmony with the music. She wished the dance could go on for ever.

The harsh, persistent shrilling of the alarm clock shattered the dream as she groped sleepily for the button. Eyes closed, she silenced its clamour and then flopped back against her pillow, trying desperately to clutch at the fading fragments of the dream. But it was no use; already the magic was disintegrating like thistledown on the wind. Outside her window the rain dripped dismally. The grey light of a February dawn drove away the warm golden mist that had enveloped her a moment ago. It was time to get up and go on duty.

Claire slid her feet over the edge of the bed and pulled on her dressing gown. No use lying there; she would only drift off to sleep again. She filled the kettle and plugged it in, gazing out of the window as she waited for it to boil. Queen Eleanor's was a new hospital, built less than five years ago in a delightful woodland setting on the outskirts of Kingsmere, a bustling East Anglian river port. In summer it was idyllic, but in winter the bare trees looked gloomy and inhospitable. It had been raining all night, by the look of it. The sky was grey, heavy with rainclouds, and the air was icy with the promise of snow later. Claire closed the window, shivered and sat down to sip her coffee. She thought again of the dream and sighed. Ever since the Christmas dance when she had spent most of the evening with Dr Simon Bonham, the new Ophthalmic Registrar, she had been unable to get him out of her mind. It had all been so romantic, meeting and being attracted like that for the first time. From the moment he had first asked her to dance, Simon had seemed unable to take his eyes off her, and everyone – including Claire – had confidently expected him to ask her out again, but since that night, not only had he been silent, but he had treated her like a complete stranger when they met. Not that they met very often; a third-year nurse didn't move in quite the same social circles as an ambitious young registrar. Anyway, ever since the New Year began she had been studying hard for her finals and she was aware that Simon too had been studying – for his Fellowship. It looked very much as though that one evening was to be the beginning and end of their romance, and that would have been fine – if only she could forget him. The way he had looked at her that evening – those intensely blue eyes; the attractive deep voice and the two strong arms that held her when they danced. If he hadn't meant to see her again why had he–

'Heavens! Aren't you even dressed yet?'

Claire jumped violently as the door behind her burst open and Maggie James burst in. Maggie had been her friend ever since they had begun their training together. She looked at Claire with anxious brown eyes.

'What's up? You're not feeling off colour, are you? You haven't got this 'flu that's going round?'

Claire shook her head. 'No, I'm fine – just slept heavily, that's all. I thought I'd have a coffee first to wake me up.'

Maggie looked at her watch. 'Better get a move on. Three more have gone sick this morning. It's my guess we're going to be rushed off our feet.'

Half an hour later they were making their way to Spencer Ward where they were both on early duty, Maggie grumbling all the while about her weight problem.

'I've had nothing but salad all weekend. Honestly, I'll be growing long ears and whiskers soon! And guess what – when I got on the scales this morning I'd actually put *on* a pound!' She glanced at her friend. 'It's not fair. You can scoff as many cream cakes as you like and it doesn't seem to make any difference.' She rolled her eyes ceilingwards. 'Whoever it was up there who organised my metabolism, I hope he's enjoying the joke!' When Claire failed to respond she looked at her again. 'Are you sure you're all right?' she asked. 'You're looking a bit peaky.'

Claire, who was still preoccupied with the tantalising dream, looked at her friend and gave herself a mental shake. 'I told you, I'm fine. I'm sorry, Maggie – what were you saying?'

Maggie shrugged resignedly. 'Never mind. It was only the usual gripe. Hardly riveting at the best of times – certainly not guaranteed to cheer up a wet Monday morning.'

Spencer Ward was men's medical and on the fourth floor. When the girls reported for duty they were met by a harassed-looking Sister Milner.

'I've just had an urgent SOS. This 'flu bug has hit some wards hard. They've only got first-year nurses left on Ophthal, so I said I'd send one of you up.' She looked at the two thoughtfully. 'I can't really spare either of you, but I suppose we'll have to manage. Well, who wants to go?' She looked from one to the other.

Maggie gave Claire a nudge. 'You go – maybe the change will do you good.'

Claire turned pink, knowing all too well what Maggie meant. Sister took up the suggestion quickly.

'Yes, now I think of it, you did do a spell on Mr Fairbrother's eye clinic in Outpatients, didn't you? Yes, you'd better go. You're the nearest thing to a staff nurse I can offer them at the moment.'

When Claire arrived on Wellington Ward she found the Sister there going quietly frantic. When she saw Claire she grasped her arm like a drowning woman clutching at a life raft.

'Oh, thank God! Here it is, ops day and not a staff nurse in sight! I've got six patients waiting for pre-med. You and I will have to cope alone.'

The next half-hour was busy. Although Sister Baker was harassed she did not let the patients see it, reassuring each of them with a quiet calm that Claire could not help but admire as they went from bed to bed. This morning's list consisted mainly of cataract removals. There was just one glaucoma case, an elderly lady who seemed particularly anxious. When they had finished Sister sent Claire back to her.

'While you've got a minute, better just look in on Miss Grainger again,' she suggested. 'Stay with her until her pre-med has taken effect.'

Claire slipped round the curtain and smiled down at the quiet figure in the bed.

'How are you feeling now, Miss Grainger?' she asked gently.

The elderly lady smiled wanly. 'Sister said the injection would make me stop worrying, but so far it isn't working.'

Claire took Miss Grainger's hand. 'Give it time. Perhaps it'll help if I stay with you for a little while. Is there anything else worrying you – apart from your operation, I mean? If I can help–'

Miss Grainger hesitated a moment. 'I am a little concerned about my poor George,' she confessed.

Claire shook her head. 'George – is he a relative? Does he live with you?'

This brought a smile to Miss Grainger's troubled face. 'Good heavens no, dear. George is my budgie – such good company, and so clever too. The trouble is, I couldn't find anyone to take him in for me, and he's all on his own, bless him. I thought I'd only be in here for a couple of days, but now they tell me it could be a week. I gave him plenty of food, but I'm afraid he might be pining for me.'

Claire patted the old lady's hand. 'Don't worry any more. Just give me your address and a key and I'll look in on him when I go off duty this evening.'

Miss Grainger's eyes lit up. 'Oh, would you, dear? There – in the locker, in my bag. You'll find an envelope addressed to me. My keys are in my purse.'

Claire found both and slipped them into the pocket of her dress, smoothing her apron over it. She looked at Miss Grainger again. She looked more relaxed now.

'Feeling better? It won't be long now – you're first on the list. In no time at all you'll be popping off to sleep, and when you wake it'll be all over.'

'Will you be here?'

'I'll be here.'

'I wish I knew just what they were going to do,' Miss Grainger murmured anxiously. 'I've asked, but no one ever tells you anything.'

Claire stole a look at the patient's chart. 'You understand what glaucoma is, don't you?'

Miss Grainger nodded. 'A pressure in the eye.'

'That's right. Your eye isn't draining properly.'

'I thought that when I had my cataract removed two years ago that would cure it,' Miss Grainger said.

'Sometimes it does. The ophthalmologist removes part of the iris at the same time and this enlarges the drainage angle. But now that you've had the lens removed it's possible for them to perform this other treatment. They freeze what's called the sclera with a tiny ice probe, and this reduces the amount of secretion–'

Before Claire could finish the curtains were whisked back and her heart almost stopped as she found herself staring up into the blue eyes of Dr Simon Bonham. This morning he was wearing horn-rimmed glasses, and the adoring smile he had bestowed upon her in her dream was replaced by a look of extreme irritation.

'Were you in charge of the signing of this consent form?' he demanded, waving it at her.

Claire shook her head. 'No. I'm not on this ward normally. I've come up from Spencer because of the–'

'Well, I wish whoever is put in charge of these things would do them efficiently. This one's improperly completed.' He elbowed Claire to one side and bent over the patient. 'How do you feel, Miss Grainger? Up to doing a little writing?' He put a hand under Claire's elbow and took her to one side. 'How long ago did she have her pre-med?'

'About fifteen minutes. It's just beginning to relax her. She was rather tense – that's why Sister asked me to stay with her.'

'And no doubt that's also the reason why you were regaling her with your limited knowledge of ophthalmology,' he remarked dryly. 'I just hope you haven't scared the life

17

out of her!' Simon Bonham turned back to the patient, his eyes concerned. 'I hate having to subject a patient to this. Just raise her up and support her for me, will you? I'm so sorry, Miss Grainger, but I have to ask you to sign here.'

A few minutes later Claire closed the curtains with a reassuring smile at Miss Grainger and followed Dr Bonham down the ward. As he pushed open the entrance doors she touched his arm.

'I was only trying to put her in the picture, Doctor,' she said. 'She was anxious because she didn't understand what was going to happen to her.'

He looked at her, one eyebrow raised cynically. 'And *you* were able to put her mind at rest, were you?'

Her chin came up. 'I think so – yes.'

He looked down at her through the rather forbidding, unfamiliar glasses. 'Perhaps you would like to explain the procedure to *me*, in that case?'

Claire took a deep breath; even when she had pulled herself up to her full height of five foot four she still had to tip her head backwards to look up at him, but she was determined not to be intimidated. She was glad she had been interested enough to read up on this particular treatment when she had worked on Mr Fairbrother's eye clinic.

'A tiny ice probe is used to freeze the ciliary body, resulting in decreased aqueous secretion,' she told him, wishing she didn't sound so much like a textbook. 'Because it affects the ciliary muscles this approach is only used on patients who have already lost their near-focusing ability or on those who have had cataract surgery.'

He took off his glasses to look at her, the ghost of a smile crinkling the corners of the blue eyes. 'Not bad, Nurse, not bad at all. All the same, I wouldn't air my cleverness on the patients too often if I were you. I daresay you've heard the saying that a little learning can be a dangerous thing.' And before she could think of a suitable witty reply she found herself looking at his retreating back as he made his way towards the lift.

Soon after that the routine of ops day began. Porters arrived with a trolley to convey Miss Grainger away to the theatre. Claire went with her as far as the lift, glad to see that the pre-med had now taken effect. She was drowsy as she waved goodbye.

When she finally had time to take a lunch break, Claire found she was hungry. Studying the canteen menu, she chose shepherd's pie with a good helping of sprouts and carrots, then with her loaded tray she looked around for somewhere to sit. The canteen was crowded, but just as she was beginning to think she would have to share with a crowd of giggling first-years she saw Maggie waving at her from a table in the far corner. When she saw what Claire had on her tray, the other girl heaved a sigh.

'Lord, I wish I'd ignored you now! All I had was salad and cottage cheese – *again!* I feel as empty as a drum, and now you're going to sit and demolish that lot in front of my starving eyes!' She peered at Claire. 'I must say you look better than you did this morning – got some colour in your cheeks now. Would it have anything to do with a certain dishy registrar who shall be nameless?'

Claire shrugged as she started to eat her shepherd's pie. 'I can't think who you mean,' she said loftily.

Maggie ignored her. 'When Sister said they wanted someone on Ophthal it seemed a heaven-sent opportunity for you.' She looked accusingly at her friend. 'Don't tell me you didn't take full advantage of the situation. You know perfectly well you've been mooning over him like a sick ferret ever since the Christmas party!'

When Claire continued eating without replying she leaned forward. 'Well? Don't be so infuriating. Did you see him – Simon Bonham?'

Claire looked up. 'Yes, I did, as a matter of fact.'

'All right, then – so what happened?'

Claire laid down her knife and fork to look levelly at Maggie. 'The moment he saw me he sank on to his knees and begged me to go out to dinner with him,' she said coolly. 'What else would he have done?'

Maggie stared at her for a moment, then pulled a face. 'You're putting me on, aren't you?'

Claire sighed. 'Of course I am. Look, Maggie, what happened at the Christmas party was obviously just the exercising of a little democracy. Simon Bonham has made it quite clear since that I'm not on his level – in any way. It was just a one-off – a friendly gesture.'

Maggie gave a disbelieving snort. 'Huh! It looked more than friendly to me – and to other people. And don't tell me *you* weren't hoping for more. You've been in a dream ever since. All I hope is that it didn't affect your finals!'

Claire gave her a warning look. 'Maggie James, if you weren't my best friend I'd tell you to go jump in the lake! I don't want to hear Simon Bonham's name any more, do you understand? And I hope you won't go around coupling my name with his either. If I hear that you have, you and I are going to fall out! I've got more on my mind than Dr Simon Bonham.'

Maggie's eyebrows shot up. 'Oh dear, it's even worse than I thought!' She smiled wryly. 'Sorry, Claire, I was only teasing really. What's up – anything I can help with?'

Claire sighed, pushing away her empty plate. 'To tell you the truth I don't know. I had a rather strange phone call from Mum last night. She wants me to go and see her this evening. She sounded really worried.'

'Do you think it's something to do with Mike?' Maggie asked.

Mike was Claire's young brother, away at boarding school. Claire shook her head. 'She didn't say, though I can't think of anything else that would make her sound so worried.'

Maggie pulled a face. 'It seems such a drain on both of you, keeping him at that posh school since your father died. There are plenty of good state schools. Couldn't he transfer to one of them?'

Claire sighed as she stirred her coffee. 'I've tried to tell you so many times, Maggie. He's a high-flier – brilliant. He has been ever since he could talk. Dad sacrificed so much to send him to St Crispin's. It's a special place for boys like Mike. He'd be hopelessly held back at an ordinary school. Mum feels she'd be letting Dad down if she took him away. It really means a lot to her, keeping him there.'

Maggie shrugged. 'Well, if you can manage–'

'We can – just,' Claire assured her. 'And if I'm lucky enough to have passed my finals things will be a little easier. As Mum says, it's been hard, but we're beginning to see some light at the end of the tunnel now.' She looked at her watch. 'Heavens, I'd better get back. Some of the patients will be coming round by now. Sister will be needing me.'

Maggie pulled a face. 'Ugh – all those post-op horrors! Give me a medical ward any day!'

As Claire had been on an early shift she had plenty of time to relax before setting out for the family home at Wytchend, a pretty suburb of Kingsmere. Her mother's job as secretary to a small firm of solicitors kept her away from the house until five-thirty. Claire was grateful for the respite. She felt weary; it had been a hard day on Ophthal.

It was while she was taking a leisurely bath that she remembered Miss Grainger's budgie. The poor old soul really was bothered about him; he was the first thing she had mentioned when she came round from the anaesthetic. Back in her room she felt in the pocket of her dress for the key and the envelope with the address and found that it was on her way. If she got off the bus two stops short of Wytchend she could make a detour quite easily.

As she dressed she wondered what was making her mother sound so worried; she wasn't given to despair or panic. Claire looked out of the window. It had stopped raining, but the sky still looked grey, and in an hour it would be dark.

Claire got off the bus and made her way towards the block of flats where Miss Grainger lived. As she climbed the stairs to the first floor she wondered why one of the neighbours couldn't have taken George in. Perhaps they were an unfriendly lot – or was it that Miss Grainger was too independent to ask?

She found number ten and let herself in with the key. George was in his cage by the window, looking really forlorn. His blue feathers drooped and he had his head tucked under one wing. His cage needed cleaning and he had eaten all the food Miss Grainger had left for him. Claire's tender heart went out to the helpless little creature. She spoke his name, chirping softly to him.

'George – hello there, I've come to feed you and clean your cage. How about that then, eh?'

George looked up and blinked at her. 'Georgie-Porgie!' he said hopefully.

But although Claire cleaned and fed him she hated leaving him alone again. It could be several more days before Miss Grainger came home and the poor little thing could die of loneliness before then. That could have a very bad effect indeed on the old lady, as quite clearly he was her sole companion. She made up her mind quickly. True, her mother was out for most of the day, but George would at least have company in the evenings, and company was obviously what he needed.

When Claire came out of the flats it had started to snow. She pulled up the collar of her red coat as she joined the bus queue.

The evening rush hour had started now, she hadn't thought of that when she had taken her time feeding George and cleaning his cage. A bus came and the queue surged forward, but as Claire was about to step on to the platform an arm shot out, barring her way.

'Sorry, can't let you on here with livestock – not with the bus crowded like this.' The belligerent conductor thrust a jutting jaw at her.

Claire stared at him. 'Livestock? But it's only a budgie!'

'Can't help that. It's standing room only and you could do someone a nasty injury with that cage. I shall have to ask you to get off.'

Claire waited ten minutes for the next bus. It was snowing quite heavily now and she was worried about George catching cold. Maybe she should have left him where he was after all! The conductor of the next bus, though marginally less aggressive, echoed the opinion of the first. Apparently she was a danger to life and limb, with her feathered companion.

She was just wondering whether to take him back to the flat when a car drew up against the kerb and a voice hailed her.

'Nurse Simms! Anything wrong? Can I help?'

Claire turned and found herself looking into Simon Bonham's face for the second time that day. She would have liked to refuse his offer of help – she would have if it hadn't been for poor George, who was looking so chilled by now that his puffed-up feathers made him appear twice his normal size.

'Oh, thanks. If you happen to be going anywhere near Wytchend – Sycamore Avenue.'

He leaned across and opened the door. 'You can direct me as we go. Better get in, I'm on a double yellow line.'

Claire settled herself in the seat next to him and struggled to do up the seat-belt, enclosing George's cage in it too. Out of the corner of his eye Simon watched her with amusement.

'Hardly the weather for taking the budgie walkies, is it?' he observed.

'It's more of a rescue operation, actually,' Claire explained. 'He belongs to Miss Grainger. She was worrying herself silly about him this morning, so I promised to look in and make sure he had enough to eat.'

Simon looked round at her in surprise.

27

'Surely she didn't mean you to take him out to dinner?'

Claire decided to ignore his attempt at flippancy. 'He looked in a bad way, so I decided to take him home to my mother. Miss Grainger hasn't anyone, you see. This bird is all she's got in the world, so it seemed to me to be rather important.'

He looked at her, his eyes serious behind the horn-rimmed glasses. 'Oh dear, I do hope you don't take all your patients' personal problems so much to heart. There is a department for that, you know.'

'I try to take an interest in all of them, just the same.'

'In my opinion it can be a mistake to become too involved,' he admonished. 'You could get weighed down by it all. Imagine how it would be if you tried to do this sort of thing for everyone. In the end you'd be quite incapable of doing your job.'

Claire deliberately ignored him. Leaning forward, she peered out into the dancing snowflakes. 'It's the next turning on the left – there, just past the letter-box. Sixty-two Sycamore Avenue.'

He drew up outside the house and turned to her. 'I'm glad I was able to help,' he told her. 'I appreciate what you're trying to do, believe me, but I still think that a nurse who can be single-minded can do a better job in the long run.'

Claire released her seat-belt and began to open the door. 'Well, perhaps we can agree to differ on that. Thank you for the lift anyway. I was just beginning to think I'd have to walk. The way those bus conductors behaved, you'd have thought George was a vulture instead of a budgie!'

He leaned across her. 'Here, let me.'

The pressure of his shoulder against hers and his breath on her cheek quickened her heart as he opened the door for her. He turned and his eyes looked into hers, and once again she marvelled at their intense blueness. She hadn't been this close to him since the night of the Christmas dance, and she held her breath. Was he about to ask her for that date after all?

'I hope you weren't too resentful at what I said to you this morning?' He looked at her enquiringly, and she looked back at him un-smilingly.

'No.'

He smiled, completely disarming her. 'Good, I knew you were far too sensible for sulks. Goodbye, then – and good luck with the rescue bid.'

Claire got out of the car and stood on the pavement. 'Goodbye – and thanks again.'

The swirling snow drove her into the shelter of the porch and she tried to quell her disappointment as she watched his car disappear into the dancing flakes. It was only as she slipped her key into the lock that she remembered her mother's anxious voice on the telephone and wondered what she was about to hear.

CHAPTER TWO

Rosemary Simms came out of the kitchen as she heard her daughter's key in the lock. She was a small, delicately built woman and it was immediately clear to any stranger that Claire took after her mother. They both had the same direct grey eyes and shining dark hair; though while Claire's tumbled about her shoulders in a curly mass, her mother's was cut in a short, boyish style that made her look considerably younger than her forty-five years.

'Darling, whatever have you got there?' asked Rosemary, drying her hands on a teatowel.

Claire held out the cage. 'He's called George, and he belongs to a patient. The poor old dear was so worried about him that I promised to look in and see that he was all right, but he looked so lonely and miserable that I decided to bring him home to you.'

Rosemary shook her head, taking George's cage and placing it on the worktop in the kitchen. 'Really, you don't get any better, do you?' she smiled affectionately at Claire. 'Ever since you could walk you've been bringing home distressed creatures.' She bent to look at George. 'He's a pretty little thing, isn't he? But do you think your patient will approve of your taking him away?'

Claire bit her lip. It was something she hadn't considered. 'Oh, I'm sure she will. I was so afraid he might die, you see, he looked so sorry for himself. She'll be in hospital for several more days. I know you're out all day, but at least he'd have someone to keep him company in the evenings–' She stopped as the smile left her mother's face.

'That was what I wanted to see you about, Claire,' Rosemary said. 'I was going to wait until after we'd eaten, but now that it's come up–'

'Now what's come up?' Claire took off her coat and hung it up in the hall, glancing over her shoulder towards her mother, who was stirring something at the stove. She could see now that there was something on her mind. She had dark circles under her eyes as though she hadn't slept properly and there was a distinct droop to her shoulders. Closing the kitchen door, Claire began to set the table.

'We are eating in here, aren't we?' she asked. 'We usually do when it's just the two of us.' She spread the cloth, waiting for her mother to continue. When she didn't she asked: 'Well, aren't you going to tell me?'

Rosemary laid down her wooden spoon and turned. 'I've been made redundant,' she announced bleakly.

Claire stared speechlessly at her mother, her hand on the cutlery drawer. 'Redundant? But you can't be! Old Mr Forbes has always said he couldn't possibly manage without you.'

'He's retiring,' Rosemary supplied. 'I know he always said he'd go on for ever, but his doctor has told him he must take it easy. He's well past retiring age and it seems his heart isn't too strong.'

Claire frowned. 'Yes, but his son – and the other partner – you've been with the firm so long. Surely they won't let you go just like that?'

Rosemary sighed and sat down at the table. 'They're going to install a computer. Of course I'll get severance pay – a lump sum, but I'm afraid that won't last long. I won't get another job at my age.'

Claire forced a laugh. 'What do you mean – at your age? Of course you will with your experience.' But Rosemary was shaking her head.

'I won't. It has to be faced, dear. What worries me is–'

'Mike's school fees,' Claire said it for her. Rosemary nodded, and the two sat staring at each other across the table.

'I lay awake most of last night, thinking about it,' said Rosemary. 'I thought if we sold the house, found a small flat – and if I took in some typing at home–'

'Oh no!' Claire looked at her mother in horror. 'You love this place. We grew up here, Mike and I. You can't sell it and move to some poky little flat! Look, Mum, if you can just hang on a few weeks the exam results will be through. If I've passed my money will be better and – I tell you what, I'll move out of the Nurses' Home and back here, then we can share expenses.'

Rosemary looked doubtful. 'But think of the travelling you'd have to do. You'd have to get up so early when you're on an early shift – and the buses are so inconvenient.'

'There's your Mini.' Claire leaned across the table. 'You won't be needing it to get to work, so I could use it.'

'I was going to sell that too.'

'This way you won't have to,' Claire told her earnestly. 'You can't give up everything, Mum. I daresay I can find someone to share the journey with so as to cut the cost.' She reached across the table to pat her mother's hand. 'Don't worry, it'll work out, you'll see. After we've eaten we'll get out a pencil and do the sums. I'm sure there are lots of small things we can cut down on without making such drastic sacrifices.'

Later that night Claire was deep in thought as she crossed the tree-fringed hospital car park. She and her mother had juggled with figures for some time after dinner and it had been clear that even with Claire's hoped-for increase in salary, cuts would have to be made in their living standards if Mike was to be kept on at his school. She had tentatively voiced Maggie's suggestion that he might be moved to a state school, but Rosemary had been adamant.

'I couldn't let him down like that, he's so happy and settled at St Crispin's. He was full of it in the Christmas holidays. And he's doing so well, you have only to read his last report. With his '0' levels in two years' time I couldn't do it to him.' She shook her head. 'But it isn't right that you should have to make sacrifices. Let me sell the house as I first suggested.'

Claire wouldn't hear of it. They were a family, all in it together, and now that she was the only breadwinner she must play her part.

A loud hooting behind her brought her out of her reverie and made her jump smartly out of the way. She turned to see Dr Steve Lang, one of the young housemen on Dr Phillips' firm, grinning at her through the wound-down window of his sports car.

'Miles away as usual!' He drew up alongside her, leaning out to touch her sleeve. 'Don't you know that it's unwise for attractive young women to go walkabout alone at this time of night?'

Claire sniffed. 'I wasn't to know you were on the prowl, was I?' she remarked tartly.

Steve winced. 'Ouch! I asked for that, didn't I?' he grinned. 'Seriously, let me walk you back to the Nurses' Home – to protect you from unknown evils.'

'And who's going to protect me from the *known* ones – like you, for instance?'

Steve parked his car and got out, grinning cheekily at her. 'That's better. When I saw you walking along with your head down, deep in thought, I began to think there was something amiss, but if you can still bite my head off there can't be too much wrong.' He took her arm and tucked it through his, looking down at her. 'You look sweet in that red coat – like a little robin, all bright-eyed and chirpy.'

Claire didn't feel particularly chirpy, but she didn't tell him so. She had known Steve since before he qualified, since she first started her training at Queen Eleanor's. He could be maddening at times, with his odd brand of humour and his persistence. There were times when his jokes came danger-ously close to disasters, but at this moment she was quite willing to have her mind taken off her troubles, even by Steve.

'I wondered if you were down with this 'flu that's going the rounds,' he said as they walked. 'I didn't see you on Spencer Ward this morning.'

She looked up into the freckled face topped with its thatch of red hair. 'No, I've been temporarily transferred to the ophthal-mic unit. They're understaffed because of illness.'

Steve coughed affectedly. 'You know, I wouldn't be surprised if I was sickening for it myself. You wouldn't like to come up and put me to bed, would you?'

Claire shook her head. 'Not a chance. I prescribe a dose of castor oil and a cold shower.'

He gave an exaggerated sigh. 'Ah, such a

cold heart for one so beautiful!' He looked at her thoughtfully for a moment. 'Ophthal, you said. I suppose that gives that upstart Bonham a chance to chat you up.'

'I'm sure Dr Bonham has better things to do than chat up the nurses,' she told him. 'You really mustn't judge everyone by yourself, Steve.'

'He didn't seem to be doing badly with you at the Christmas dance,' he retorted. 'You were supposed to be there with me, but you danced with him all evening. I still owe him for that!'

'You know perfectly well that I wasn't *with* you – or with anyone else either for that matter,' Claire rebuked him. 'I do wish you'd stop giving everyone the impression that we're a couple.'

He sighed gustily. 'Don't take my dreams away,' he pleaded dramatically. 'Let me at least have those.'

Claire shrugged off his arm. 'If you're going to be silly you can leave me here and now,' she told him crossly. 'I'm not in the mood.'

'Sorry – just trying to cheer you up. What is it – trooble at t'mill?' She nodded and he squeezed her arm. 'Make me a cup of coffee and tell me all about it. I promise to behave.'

She shook her head.

'Not tonight, Steve – I'm on an early in the morning, I must get to bed. Maybe I'll see you tomorrow.'

Steve put his hands on her shoulders, turning her to face him. 'One small good night peck, then? Not much to ask, is it?'

Claire began to shake her head, trying to free herself from his firm grip, but the next moment she found herself in his arms, being soundly kissed. She struggled, protesting as a car swung into the car park, its strong headlights spotlighting them.

'Why can't you ever take no for an answer?' she snapped angrily as the car swept past, making a soft swishing sound in the freshly fallen snow. She heard Steve chuckle and looked at him enquiringly.

'What's so funny?'

'That'll show him,' he said.

'Show who?'

'Bonham– Didn't you recognise that car of his?'

Back in her room Claire sank on to the bed. Steve really was the limit! It wasn't her day. Simon must think her a perfect idiot. First he had discovered her freezing to death at the bus queue with Miss Grainger's budgie, then he had to witness her undignified struggle with Steve! Any good first impression she might have made must be completely obliterated by now. Just for the moment even the worry of her mother's redundancy was forgotten.

The door opened a crack and Maggie's face looked round it. She had a towel wrapped round her head turban-fashion.

'Ah, I was washing my hair and I thought I heard your footsteps in the corridor. Mind if I come in?' She slipped inside and closed the door behind her. 'You all right?' she asked, peering at Claire. 'You haven't even taken your coat off.'

Claire stood up wearily and removed her coat, crossing to the cupboard to hang it up. 'My mother's been made redundant from her job,' she said flatly. 'It means we'll have to cut down. I shall have to go home to live, for a start.'

Maggie frowned. 'Oh no – all that travelling? All this is to keep Mike the wonder child on at school, I suppose?' When Claire didn't reply she went on: 'Well, you know what I think about it, so I won't say it again.'

'You really don't know what you're talking about, so please don't,' Claire snapped, then relented as Maggie's goodnatured face dropped. 'Oh, look, it'll be all right. I shall

40

have the use of Mum's Mini and I'm going to put a notice on the board tomorrow, offering lifts on a sharing basis – then, if I'm lucky enough to have passed my finals– We've worked it all out and we can manage all right.'

'You know, if I hadn't met him I'd imagine Mike to be a spoilt little horror,' said Maggie, sinking on to a chair. 'If I didn't know what a nice child he is–' She shrugged, leaving the sentence unfinished. 'What do you think *he'll* feel like when he knows that you and your mother are going without to educate him?'

'With a bit of luck he never *will* know,' Claire said stoically.

'But if he does find out–' Maggie shook her head, 'he'll feel guilty for the rest of his life. I don't think it's right. If he's as brainy as you say, surely he'll do well wherever he studies.'

'Oh, for heaven's sake shut up, Maggie!' Claire erupted. 'I've had quite enough today, one way and another. It's all fixed, so that's that.'

Maggie suddenly grinned. 'Want a coffee? Put your feet up and I'll make it for you, then we'll talk about something else. I can bore you with the latest about my diet. I've

41

found this new one – you eat nothing but bananas for three days! It's supposed to shed pounds!'

The two ended the evening in laughter as Claire recounted her embarrassing adventures in the bus queue and later in Simon Bonham's car with George, the budgie. Somehow Maggie had a knack of showing up the funny side of things. She even managed to make light of the galling business of being seen struggling with Steve in the car park, insisting that Simon couldn't have recognised her, but later, as Claire lay staring into the darkness, sleep eluding her, she felt quite sure that he must have. The bright red coat was a dead giveaway. Her last thoughts as she fell asleep should have been about her future as sole family breadwinner, the responsibility for which sat heavily on her young shoulders. But the last image that occupied her mind as she drifted into oblivion was Simon's face; the intensely blue eyes and crisply waving brown hair; the way her heart had quickened when he had leaned across to open the car door for her, hoping that at last he was about to ask her for a date. But she might as well have cried for the moon. Clearly he would never ask her out now. He had had a perfect opportunity this evening, but his manner towards her had been – she furrowed her brow, trying to think of the right phrase – polite, almost patronising. Yes, definitely patronising. She began to wonder if she had imagined the romance of their meeting at the Christmas dance. And now, after he had seen her making a complete fool of herself in the car park, there seemed little chance that he would ever think of her as anything but a featherbrained idiot.

As soon as she went on duty the following morning Claire walked down the ward to Miss Grainger's bed. The old lady sat up, drinking her morning tea and looking considerably better than she had the day before. When she saw Claire she smiled.

'Good morning, dear.'

Claire felt in her pocket and produced the keys to Miss Grainger's flat. 'Here are your keys. I'll put them in your handbag, shall I? I went to see George last night. I hope you don't mind, but he looked so lonely that I took him home to my mother. She'll look after him for you till you go home again.'

Miss Grainger smiled. 'Oh, how kind! I didn't mean you to go to so much trouble.'

'That's quite all right.' Claire took the

empty cup from the old lady's hand. 'Now, I'll put your drops in for you, shall I? How does the eye feel?'

By breakfast time the whole ward knew about Claire's errand of mercy the previous evening, and after the first morning rush was over Sister eyed her icily.

'I'd like a word with you in my office, Nurse Simms,' she said. Claire followed her inside and closed the door, wondering what had happened to make her look so stern. Sister sat at her desk and motioned her to take the chair opposite.

'I understand that you have taken it upon yourself to go to a patient's home,' she said frostily.

Claire nodded. 'She was worried. I–'

'Not only that,' Sister interrupted, 'but you apparently saw fit to remove something belonging to her.'

'Her budgie,' Claire put in. 'She was worried about him, so I said I'd look in on my way home. He really looked sad, so I took him to my mother. I don't see–'

'I'm surprised at you!' Sister shook her head. 'After three years of training, you surely know that you should never involve yourself personally with a patient. If you were concerned you should have got in

44

touch with the hospital social worker. I'm sure you are well aware of that.'

'I didn't think they'd have time to bother with a budgie. Besides, there wasn't time,' Claire protested. 'The poor little thing looked as though he might expire.'

'And supposing he does?'

The question brought Claire up short. It was something she hadn't even considered. She stared speechlessly at Sister.

'You realise, of course, that you have now made yourself personally responsible?'

'I – I'm sure he'll be all right,' said Claire in a small voice.

Sister rose from her desk. 'I sincerely hope for your sake that you're right,' she said. 'Obviously you didn't stop to consider what repercussions your action might have. Suppose there were a break-in and something of value were to be stolen? You would automatically come under suspicion. In future I advise you to try to be less impulsive. Now I'd like you to get on. We have a great deal to do before doctor's rounds. There's a new admission in bed four, a young woman with severely infected corneal burns of both eyes.' Sister pulled down the corners of her mouth. 'I believe she's been using an ultra-violet sun lamp without wearing goggles.

Some people never learn, do they?'

When Mr Fairbrother came up to the ward to do his round, accompanied by Simon, Claire glanced at him speculatively. Had Sister heard about her rescue operation from the other patients in the ward, or had he told her? She tried to catch his eye, but he avoided her, treating her with an icy formality that made her heart sink. He must have seen her with Steve last night and gathered quite the wrong impression.

In her lunch break Claire couldn't find Maggie anywhere. She asked one of the other nurses from Spencer Ward and was told that she hadn't reported for duty that morning. Hurrying across to the Nurses' Home, she tapped on Maggie's door. From within came a croaking squeak:

'Come in.'

Maggie lay in bed looking hot and heavy-eyed. 'What's wrong?' asked Claire. 'Are you ill?'

Maggie pulled herself into a half sitting position and then flopped weakly back. 'It's some sort of bug. I was fine last night when I went to bed, as you know, but I woke in the early hours with a sore throat, aching all over. I couldn't even stagger to the tele-phone this morning to call Sister.'

'Poor old love!' Claire laid a hand on the burning forehead, then began to tidy the rumpled bed. 'Have you had anything – a drink – food?' she asked. Maggie shook her head. 'Right, I'll get you something.' She plugged in the electric kettle, then opened the other girl's cupboard. 'Have you got any aspirin? That's quite a temperature you've got.'

Maggie shook her head. 'I never need it as a rule.'

'Let's have a look at that throat.'

Maggie opened her mouth obligingly to reveal red, angry-looking tonsils.

Claire winced. 'Oh dear, that does look nasty! I think you should see a doctor.'

Maggie shook her head vigorously. 'We're so short-staffed. I don't want to be off any longer than I can help. Look, do you think you could get hold of some Paracetamol for me? I know a couple of doses would put me on my feet again – I'm as strong as a horse.'

Claire shook her head. 'I don't know– You really should be properly diagnosed. We're supposed to report 'flu, you know that.'

'Oh, don't be stuffy! It isn't as bad as all that.' Maggie pulled a face. 'Go on, Claire. I'm disgustingly healthy, you know I am. A couple of days' rest and I'll be as right as rain. It's only a bug. I'll phone Sister later and tell her I've got a bad headache.'

Claire shook her head. 'Well – I don't know–'

Maggie frowned. 'Look, Claire, I've got a date on Monday with Guy Phelps, that dishy new physio. I'll die if I can't go.'

'Oh, all right then,' Claire said doubtfully. 'But stay in bed till your temperature goes down, won't you – promise?'

Maggie grinned. 'Promise.'

'Okay – I'll try to get back to you later.' She made Maggie a hot drink and a sandwich, then hurried back to the main block again, calling in at the pharmacy on her way, but to her dismay she found it closed for the weekend. Of course, she had forgotten that it was Saturday.

Just before the afternoon visiting hour Sister beckoned her into the office and unlocked the drugs cupboard.

'Mr Fairbrother has prescribed antibiotic drops for the corneal burns in bed four,' she said, 'and anaesthetic drops for the pain. They came up from Pharmacy just before lunch. Better start them now, before the visitors come. The left eye is the worst and she's to have it patched. Just see to it, will you?'

'Yes, Sister.' Claire was scanning the cupboard. There on the top shelf was a large jar of Paracetamol tablets.

'During visiting hour I shall be leaving you in charge,' Sister was saying. 'I have to slip down to see the SNO – this 'flu epidemic is reaching crisis proportions. There's talk of getting some agency nurses in next week. I shouldn't be too long. Can you cope?'

Claire nodded. 'Yes, of course I can.'

'Well, you know where I'll be if you want me.'

Claire sat at the ward desk and watched as the visitors arrived, laden with their assortment of bulging paper bags, flowers and bottles of squash. When they were all settled she rose, heart in mouth, and slipped into Sister's office. Her heartbeat quickened as she unlocked the drugs cupboard and took down the bottle of tablets. She counted out six – that should be enough till the pharmacy opened on Monday. She wrapped them in a tissue and slipped them into her pocket, then, replacing the cap of the jar, she lifted it back on to the shelf, closing and locking the door with a sigh of relief.

'Nurse Simms, what on *earth* do you think you're doing?'

She spun round, red-faced, her heart

hammering guiltily, and found herself face to face with Steve Lang. 'Oh, you scared the life out of me!' she told him. 'What are you doing up here anyway?'

'I came to see you,' he told her. 'I was bothered about you. You didn't seem quite yourself last night.' He frowned. 'It seems I was right to be worried. What was that you took from the cupboard?'

She shook her head. 'I didn't. I was just checking—' He stepped forward and took her arm. 'Don't bluff, Claire. I saw you – watched you wrap some tablets up and hide them in your pocket. That's serious, you know.'

'Oh, it *isn't!* They're only Paracetamol for Maggie,' she told him. 'She's got a sore throat.'

He stared at her. 'I hope you're not in the habit of taking drugs and passing them round your friends like sweets?'

'Of course I'm not! What do you take me for?' she demanded angrily. 'It's the first time I've ever done such a thing – and it was against my better judgment. Maggie just wanted to get back to work as soon as she could, that's all.'

'Then why didn't she see a doctor?' he asked.

Claire had no answer. She lifted her shoulders helplessly.

'I really should report it, you know.'

She raised her eyes disbelievingly to his. 'Steve! You wouldn't?'

He shook his head. 'What you say might well be true – on the other hand it could be a bunch of lies.'

'You know me better than that.' She looked hard at him, trying to assess his mood. It wasn't always easy to tell when Steve was joking. But he seemed in deadly earnest as he said:

'There was a case a few years back, apparently. A nurse had got into serious debt, and she was stealing barbs and selling them outside to pay her creditors off. The trouble was that she wasn't able to stop. The people she was selling to threatened to spill the beans on her if she stopped supplying them. It was a vicious circle. She's serving a prison sentence now.'

Claire laughed nervously. '*Steve!* Stop trying to frighten me. I told you, all I've got is a few Paracetamol tablets. I'd have got them from the pharmacy, only they were closed for the weekend. I'll show you if you like.'

'No,' he laid a hand on her arm, 'don't be

51

a fool. I believe you, of course.' He rubbed his chin, regarding her thoughtfully. 'I mean it, though, Claire. It puts me in a difficult position. Not only are you covering up what might be a case of 'flu but stealing drugs as well. And now you've made me an accessory.'

She lifted her chin, her grey eyes defiant as they looked into his. 'All right, then, if that's how you feel, you'd better go ahead and report me.'

He shook his head. 'I'd hate to see you get into trouble when your exam results are just about to come through. I know you want to stay on at Queen Eleanor's. Maybe I could help, though. There is a favour you can do me. Perhaps we could help each other.'

Claire was thinking fast. If Steve really did report her, and she was turned down for a permanent post – She shuddered, refusing to think of the complications that could cause.

'All right,' she said, looking up at him, 'you'd better tell me what it is?'

He patted her cheek. 'Atta girl! Not here, though. I'll see you this afternoon when you come off duty – in the coffee-shop down-stairs – right?'

CHAPTER THREE

'You *have* to be joking!' Claire stared at Steve across the plastic-topped table where they sat in a quiet corner of the visitors' coffee-shop.

He shook his head. 'I'm not. It really would save me a lot of aggro, Claire. Go on, be a pal – it's only one Sunday afternoon.'

'I'm on duty.' Claire was clutching at straws and she knew it wouldn't be any use.

'You're off at four. There'd be plenty of time.'

'It's blackmail!' she accused.

He grinned. 'That's rather an exaggeration.'

'It's deceitful at best.'

Steve pulled a wry face. 'So is stealing from the drugs cupboard.'

She gave an exasperated little snort. 'I wish you wouldn't keep calling it that! I've explained it all to you.'

'Nevertheless–' His look said everything, and Claire gave in helplessly. She wouldn't put anything past him; there were times when he could be totally amoral.

She sighed resignedly. 'Oh, all right then, if you really think you can pull the wool over your mother's eyes. But I warn you, I can't promise to be convincing as your fiancée.'

He leaned across the table and took her hand. 'Ah, but that's part of the agreement. If you fail to convince, the deal is off. You see, my mother, bless her heart, is obsessed by the idea that marriage would "settle me down", as she so quaintly puts it. Your job is to assure her that you're the kind of girl who will do just that.'

Claire glared at him coldly. 'You do know, don't you, Steve, that I wouldn't marry you if you were the last man on earth?' She sighed. 'You're a prize rat, do you know that?'

He smiled sweetly at her. 'Flattery will get you everywhere, sweetheart. Just keep talking to me in that way and I'm sure my mother will take you to her heart! Your sentiments are hers to a T!'

She chewed her lip. 'Just one Sunday afternoon, you said?'

'Just the one.'

'But what if she wants to see me again?'

Steve shook his head. 'You can leave that to me. If you're convincing enough once should be enough to put her off the scent for a while.'

She capitulated. 'What time, then?'

'I'll pick you up at about four-thirty. And I suggest you wear your red coat. It gives you an air of vulnerable innocence – like Little Red Riding Hood.'

Claire rose from the table and fastened her cloak at the neck, glaring at him as she did so. 'No prizes for guessing the identity of the wolf!' she said dryly.

They parted at the main entrance doors and Claire began to make her way across the inner court to the Nurses' Home. In the pocket of her dress she still had the Paracetamol tablets for Maggie. She hoped wryly that they did the trick, after all she had gone through – and still had to go through – in order to get them!

The weather had improved slightly since the previous evening, but the snow had turned to slush, turning the flowerbeds in the court into muddy mounds. As she skirted the puddles Claire wondered what she could have done to deserve the mess she seemed to have got herself into. As though her own family problems weren't enough, she now found herself enmeshed in Steve's. He had driven her right into a corner – and all over a few Paracetamol tablets for Maggie! She hoped her efforts would be appreciated. Heaven only knew what complications might arise from tomorrow afternoon's escapade, knowing Steve!

'Nurse Simms – Claire!'

She stopped as hands caught her by the shoulders. She had been so deep in thought that she hadn't seen Simon coming towards her across the court and had almost collided with him.

He smiled down at her. 'Steady! Are you all right? You were miles away there.'

'I'm fine – tired, I suppose. Sorry.'

He hesitated. 'I hope nothing went wrong with your rescue bid last night?'

Claire shrugged. If only Miss Grainger's budgie were all she had to worry about! 'No, George is fine, thank you,' she said politely. 'Except that Sister got to hear about what I did and gave me a rocket this morning.'

He frowned. 'Oh dear – I gather it's been one of those days. I thought you were looking a bit down.' Again he hesitated, then asked impulsively: 'Look, are you doing anything this evening?'

She stared at him in amazement. 'Well, no.'

'Then come and have dinner with me. You

56

really do look as though you could do with a change.'

Claire's chin went up proudly. 'You don't have to feel sorry for me. I eat quite regularly, actually.'

He looked surprised for a moment, then laughed. 'Is that the way it sounded? Seriously, I would like you to come. Look – a colleague of mine was coming over to eat with me this evening, but something has come up and the arrangement is off. I'd already booked a table at The Sailmaker's, that new place near the docks. It seems a shame to waste it, so what do you say?'

Inside, her heart was racing. Simon was actually asking her out! Wasn't that all she had been dreaming about for the past six weeks? But now, perversely, she was half tempted to hand him a haughty refusal.

When it finally came out, her acceptance sounded cool. 'Well, thank you – as long as you've already booked the table.'

He smiled down at her in the disarming way that made her heart turn over. 'It would be nice to think you wanted to as well – just a little?' He looked at her enquiringly and a stab of resentment jabbed at her. Really – men! They seemed to expect such a lot. At the Christmas dance he'd been so attentive, leading her – and everyone else – to believe he was really attracted to her, yet ever since – nothing! What did he want her to do – grovel?

'What time shall I expect you?' she asked, ignoring his last remark.

He looked at his watch. 'Shall we say eight o'clock? That will give us time for a drink first.'

Claire watched as he went on his way, his white coat unbuttoned as usual and flapping in the wind. What was it about him that she found so attractive? Obviously his good looks were all that women found ideal, but she knew at least a dozen men who were just as attractive in that way. There was something more, something about his personality – small mannerisms, the way the rather serious blue eyes suddenly lit up when he smiled, the small flashes of humour that lifted his eyebrows and the corners of his mouth. She wondered what could be behind his seemingly cavalier attitude, half wishing now that she had refused his invitation.

'Hey! Look where you're going, can't you?'

The angry warning came too late as Claire cannoned smack into a porter who was coming out of the building, manoeuvring a trolley loaded with cardboard boxes.

'Oh – sorry!' She stooped to help him pick up those that had fallen off, wondering wryly if she was flirting with disaster, going out with Simon tonight. It certainly hadn't been her lucky day so far!

Maggie was sitting up in bed, reading a magazine and looking much better. She looked up as Claire walked in.

'Oh, there you are. I was beginning to wonder where you'd got to.'

Claire pulled off her cloak and cap and flopped into a chair. 'It's been quite a day, one way and another.' She felt in her pocket. 'Here are your tablets, though I must say you're looking better already.'

'No thanks to you,' said Maggie, reaching for an apple and taking a bite out of it. 'If I'd waited for you I could have expired by now. After you'd gone I went down the corridor and knocked Jill up – I suddenly remembered she was on nights. You know what a hypochondriac she is. She fixed me up with everything – aspirin, throat pastilles, the lot. She even went out and bought me some fruit. Now that's what I *call* a friend.'

Claire stared at her. 'You mean I've gone to the trouble of getting you these for nothing?'

59

Maggie blinked uncomprehendingly. 'Trouble? What trouble could you possibly have getting me a couple of Paracetamols?'

Claire opened her mouth and then closed it again, making for the door. She decided to say nothing. She felt as though she'd been explaining all day, and where had it got her? If she hurried she'd have time to wash her hair and have a bath. She deserved to be taken out this evening and she meant to enjoy herself.

To say that The Sailmaker's was 'near the docks' wasn't quite accurate. It stood a little further along the waterfront, nearer to the mouth of the estuary. As the name suggested, it had once been the premises of a sailmaker, in the days when the flourishing river port of Kingsmere was haven to a host of sailing ships and barges carrying coal and grain.

Simon parked the car and came round to open the door for Claire. Although an icy wind blew in from the sea she could not resist stopping for a moment to savour the beauty of the dark, silken water flowing past, reflecting the lights on the river bank. On the other side of the estuary more lights twinkled, and as she stood there, a large ship sailed past, engines throbbing, on its way out to sea. She could just make out the name on the hull: *Helga Braun*, and underneath: *Hamburg*. She sighed.

'I can never see them without wishing I were going too,' she said wistfully.

Simon laughed. 'Think what it must be like keeping watch in the small hours with a force eight gale blowing and icy rain cutting into your face!'

Inside, the restaurant was warm and welcoming. The new owner had restored the centuries-old building with taste and imagination, exposing the ancient timbers and using the space cleverly.

The table they were shown to was in a deep bay, overlooking the river. Claire settled herself comfortably on the green velvet banquette, smiling at Simon.

'Your friend doesn't know what he's missing.'

Simon looked at her, taking in the glossy curls that bounced on her shoulders, the cream angora dress that accentuated her slim figure, and smiled. 'How right you are!'

Claire looked away. 'It's nice to get away, isn't it? Life at Queen Eleanor's is pretty hectic at the moment with all the 'flu and—' She broke off, catching his appraising look.

She blushed and turned her eyes towards the menu he handed her.

'What will you have?' The expression was quite gone now as he studied his own menu. 'I can recommend the fish here. It's literally sea-fresh.'

The moment had passed, but it left Claire puzzled. Just for a moment he had looked at her as he had on the night they first met.

He looked up and caught her looking at him. 'All right?' he asked, raising an enquiring eyebrow.

She blushed. 'It's just – you're not wearing your glasses tonight,' she blurted, catching gratefully at a straw. 'I wondered–'

He smiled. 'Contact lenses,' he explained briefly. 'I only wear the others when I'm working with patients. I always think it projects a more reassuring image somehow.'

The meal was as good as he had promised, and as they sat with their coffee and the brandy Simon had persuaded her to have they watched as more ships sailed on the tide, cruising majestically past the overhanging bay where they sat, which, they discovered, had once been the sailmaker's loading platform.

Simon smiled at her. 'Do you still wish you were going with them?' he asked.

Claire shook her head. 'Not now, I'm far too relaxed and comfortable.' She didn't tell him that at this moment she wouldn't have changed places with anyone else in the world.

He looked at his watch. 'I suppose I should be getting you back. I take it you're still on the early shift?'

She nodded regretfully, gathering up her gloves and handbag. 'That's right.'

Outside she pulled up the collar of her coat and Simon looked at her. 'Are you cold? If not I thought you might like to walk. The fresh air will help you to sleep.'

She nodded enthusiastically, and he took her arm as they walked along the dockside.

'Kingsmere must be very pleasant in summertime,' Simon remarked.

'It is. Winter will soon be over,' Claire replied. 'Time goes so quickly.' She glanced at him out of the corner of her eye. 'It doesn't seem five minutes since Christmas.'

He looked down at her. 'It was rather a good party, wasn't it?'

'Yes.'

As they walked on the silence between them changed subtly. Now it was charged with tension. She wondered if he would offer an explanation for his apparent lack of interest in her since that evening, but as they walked, looking out over the dark water, he said nothing. His expression was enigmatic. Suddenly he stopped and leaned his arms on the sea wall, looking thoughtful.

As she joined him her arm brushed against his. He turned and their eyes met. She didn't know quite how it happened, but the next moment she was in his arms, his mouth on hers, and everything else was forgotten in the breathless beating of her heart as he kissed her. As he released her she shivered.

'You're cold.' He looked down at her. 'We must be mad, standing here in sub-zero temperatures!' He smiled, brushing back a strand of hair blown across her face by the wind. 'Come back to the flat with me, I'll make you some coffee to warm you.' When she hesitated he smiled, holding her away from him to study her expression. 'What are you afraid of – losing your beauty sleep?'

Claire buried her face against his shoulder. How could she tell him she was in greater fear of losing her head and heart than a few trivial hours of sleep? Yet nothing could have kept her from going with him.

Simon's flat was the top floor of an elegant Georgian house only minutes from Queen Eleanor's. In dreamy moments Claire had often wondered how he lived; speculated on his taste in furnishings, his likes and dislikes, but when he unlocked the door and ushered her in she was surprised to see that it was not at all as she had imagined. Although it was adequately furnished there was a bareness about it, a feeling of transience, as though it were a temporary home with most of the owner's possessions still packed away. It gave no hint of the occupier's personality at all. As she stood looking around her Simon smiled, guessing at her thoughts.

'Not very tasteful, is it? I haven't had a place of my own before – always lived in hospital accommodation. I'm not used to home-making.' He laughed. 'But give me time. When I get round to it I'm going to start buying all those glossy magazines that tell you what goes with what. The trouble is, I never seem to get the time for things like that.'

'It could be very nice,' she said, then blushed at the unintentional implication that it wasn't already. 'I mean, I'm sure you'll make a marvellous job of it.'

He smiled wryly. 'Well, I'd like to think so too, but I can't say I have much confidence.' He held out his hand. 'Give me your coat, then I'll make some coffee.'

She slipped it off and handed it to him. 'Can I help?'

'You can come into the kitchen,' he told her. 'That's the one place I'm not ashamed of. At least I know how to keep the place clean.'

He was right. The kitchen was small but well equipped and neat. Simon also seemed to have collected a number of gadgets to make catering for himself easy. There was a microwave oven, a food processor and a coffee maker, which he now filled and switched on as Claire watched.

'The milk is in the fridge,' he told her over his shoulder. 'And you'll find a saucepan in the cupboard under the sink.'

She opened the fridge and took out a bottle with about half an inch of milk at the bottom of it. 'This seems to be all there is.' She held it out to him and his jaw dropped.

'Damn! I remember now – I meant to buy some on my way home. Look, my neighbour always has some to spare, I'll just go up and ask him. I shan't be a moment – if you wouldn't mind getting the cups out. You'll find them in the cupboard there.'

He paused as he passed her, reaching out to cup her chin with his hand: smiling down into her eyes in that disarming way of his. 'Now you know my secret, don't you?'

'Secret?' Claire looked up at him breathlessly.

He laughed. 'Yes. Now you know how disorganised I am!' He bent to brush his lips across hers, making her heart turn a double somersault.

When he had gone she found a tray and set out the cups on it. She was just looking for some sugar when the telephone rang in the other room. She paused for a moment, then went to answer it.

'Hello. Dr Bonham's flat.'

A woman's voice answered. It was deep and musical and it sounded slightly surprised. 'Oh – is Simon there?'

'He isn't at the moment. Can I take a message?'

The woman hesitated. 'Perhaps you'd ask him to ring me when he has a moment,' she said. 'It isn't urgent or anything, I'd just like to speak to him.'

'Of course.' As she searched for a pad and pencil Claire felt curiosity gnawing at her. Who *was* this woman, and why did she want to speak to Simon? There didn't seem to be a pencil on the telephone table, so she opened a drawer and looked inside. There, under a jumble of odds and ends, was a photograph. She drew it out. Smiling up at her out of a handsome silver frame was a girl. She was beautiful, a cloud of auburn hair framing a heart-shaped face out of which smiled enormous green eyes. Scrawled across it in a flamboyant hand were the words: 'To darling Simon, with all my love, till death us do part – Sally.'

For a moment it was as though time were suspended. As she stared down at the lovely face Claire forgot everything, even the caller, until the receiver crackled in her hand, reminding her of what she had been about to do. Quickly she picked up a pen she found in the drawer.

'Can you give me your name, please?'

'He'll know who it is,' the woman said, 'he was expecting me to ring. Just ask him to ring me when he has time. He knows the number.'

Claire dropped the receiver back on to its rest, still staring at the face in the photograph. Was she looking at the owner of the voice on the telephone? The sudden silence that filled the room seemed charged with electricity. Had Simon intended to bring her back to the flat and deliberately hidden the photograph away? Was the mysterious Sally the reason for his coolness since their first meeting? Could it have been she who had let him down this evening? Was she – Claire – a way of getting back at her, making her jealous?

When Simon opened the door and came back into the room she was startled, swinging round almost guiltily.

'Oh, it's you!'

He grinned. 'Who were you expecting? I got the milk. Have–' He was stopped in mid-sentence by the telephone ringing again. Claire stood aside and he stepped forward, reached for the receiver, handing her the bottle of milk.

'Dr Bonham speaking.'

After a moment he replaced it and turned to her with a rueful expression. 'I've got to go, I'm afraid,' he told her. 'An accident on the A47. One of the victims has glass fragments in the eye. It could be nasty.' He bent to kiss her briefly. 'Do you want to wait for me? Someone should drink the coffee after all the trouble I've gone to to get the milk.'

She shook her head. 'No, I'd better get back.'

He smiled regretfully. 'I daresay you're right. You know how it is with accidents –

I'll be lucky if the glass fragments are all I find waiting for me! I'll drop you off on the way.'

In the car on the way back to the hospital Claire was silent. She felt utterly miserable, unable to think of anything to say that wouldn't give away her frame of mind. As Simon drew up outside the Nurses' Home he looked at her.

'I'm sorry the evening had to be cut short, darling. We must go out again some time soon.' He reached across her to open her door and his cheek brushed hers, its slight roughness quickening her heart. Abruptly, she pushed the door open and turned away from him.

'Perhaps we could – perhaps your *friend* will stand you up again!' The moment she had said it she bit her lip hard. Damn! After all her studied coolness he had shown her hand – shown that she cared about his cavalier treatment. She made to get out of the car, but he caught at her arm, holding her fast.

'Claire, what's the matter? You're angry.'

She wouldn't look at him. 'Please let me go. You're hurting my arm,' she said in a small voice.

He let go her arm immediately. 'I'm sorry.

Look, I can't stop now. We'll talk tomorrow.'

'There's no need.' She slipped out of the car. 'Thank you for the dinner,' she muttered. 'Good night.'

For a brief moment he hesitated, then, without another word, he let in the clutch and drove on. It was only as she watched him go that she remembered – she hadn't given him the telephone message.

CHAPTER FOUR

Claire lay awake for a long time that night, trying to make sense of what had happened between her and Simon. Had he really been so sure that she would go back to the flat with him this evening? And who was Sally? Quite clearly she was someone who played a major part in Simon's life. The words scrawled across the photograph were etched deeply on Claire's mind: 'Till death us do part.' She must be the fiancée – perhaps even the *wife* he had left behind in the Midlands town he had come from. It explained everything – the reason Simon hadn't asked her out again after the Christmas dance, his whole attitude towards her. She fumed inwardly. If he thought he could use her to make this other girl jealous, walk all over her emotions with little or no regard – well, he'd chosen the wrong person!

But soon her anger had dissolved into hurt and disappointment and she swallowed hard at the tears that threatened. It really had been the most awful day. A good thing she would have plenty to occupy her during the coming weeks, plenty to keep her mind off Simon and his heartless two-timing. If it hadn't been for that telephone call– She buried her face in the pillow, burning with shame at the eager way she had responded to Simon's kiss. Well, at least she had been saved from making a bigger fool of herself. That was something to be thankful for!

When she went on duty the following morning she found that she was being shunted round yet again. The staff situation had eased on Ophthal, but now, with Maggie away, there was an acute shortage of staff on Spencer. When she arrived there Claire found Sister Milner fully occupied with an emergency admission, a young man in a diabetic coma. Claire found herself thrown immediately into action, standing by to help the registrar who was putting the patient on a drip.

Later, as Dr Phillips the consultant left, leaving instructions that they should contact him as soon as the patient recovered consciousness, Sister shook her head.

'Some people never learn,' she grumbled. 'He must have been having symptoms for at least the past twelve hours. It seems his mother was out for the day. He was in bed when she got home last night and this morning she found him unconscious.'

'Perhaps he's a fairly recent case,' Claire suggested. 'With his mother being out for the day he probably forgot his insulin injection.'

Sister shrugged. 'He'll have to learn, then, won't he? It's hardly fair on his poor mother. Ketoacidosis isn't funny for anyone concerned. You'd better keep an eye on him until he comes round, though heaven knows there's enough to do.'

Claire found herself once more 'acting staff' as she bustled about the morning tasks, in charge of the less experienced nurses. It would be ironic if she hadn't passed her finals after this, she told herself wryly. Every so often she peeped round the curtains of the diabetic patient and about an hour later was rewarded by a flickering of his eyelids. She went to fetch Sister, who made a brief examination.

'Yes, he's coming round all right,' she confirmed. 'I'll ring Dr Phillips at once.' She glanced at Claire. 'Stay with him till I get back, and try to remember anything he might say. It could be important.'

Claire sat down at the young man's bedside, watching him carefully. She was trying hard to remember all she had learned on the subject of diabetes. Most of the patients she had come into contact with seemed to manage their condition very well. This was the first time she had seen a case of ketoacidosis and she was curious to know how it had come about.

The patient couldn't have been more than eighteen, and when he opened his eyes she saw that they were brown. As he took in his surroundings they widened with apprehension.

'Where am I?' he asked anxiously. 'I didn't conk out, did I?'

Claire smiled at his choice of words. At least he hadn't suffered any brain damage. She reached out to pat his hand reassuringly.

'You're going to be fine. The doctor's on his way up to see you. Can you remember what happened?'

He frowned. 'Mum was out for the day – it was the Women's Institute outing. I must have eaten something that disagreed with me, because I was sick. It started about ten o'clock, soon after I'd had my injection. I got worried because I didn't know how it would affect my insulin level. I didn't like to ring the doc on Saturday morning, they only deal with emergencies at the surgery, so I rang a pal of mine whose married sister is diabetic, and he told me I should stop the insulin completely.'

Claire gasped. 'You really should have checked! It was the worst thing you could have done. You should have made yourself a large glass of squash and kept sipping it. Even if you kept on vomiting that would have kept up your blood sugar level.'

He gave her a disarming grin. 'Thanks, Nurse, I'll remember that.' He looked at the drip in his arm. 'How long do I have to be hooked up to this contraption?'

Claire didn't have a chance to answer him, for the curtains were drawn aside and Dr Phillips slipped inside, accompanied by Sister. Briefly, Claire told them what she had just learned from the patient. Dr Phillips shook his head.

'Oh dear, oh dear – heaven preserve me from well-meaning friends! There *are* rare occasions when insulin must be stopped, but you must always get qualified advice another time.' He prepared to make the routine tests.

'Well, I shall know what to do next time I get a stomach upset,' the patient announced. 'Nurse here tells me I should have kept on sipping a glass of squash to keep up my blood sugar level.'

Both Sister and Dr Phillips turned to look at Claire, who felt a slow flush creeping up her neck. Dr Phillips smiled.

'Well, Nurse,' he said quietly, 'it's gratifying to know that some of you *do* listen to the lectures!'

After that the rest of the shift was fairly routine, though with the shortage of staff there was enough to keep Claire busy. When she came off duty she would dearly have loved to put her feet up and her heart sank when she remembered her date with Steve. How on earth was she going to pretend to be his fiancée? The whole idea was quite mad. Trust Steve to think of it! For two pins she would have called his bluff, but she couldn't quite trust him not to spill the beans over her petty rifling of the drugs cupboard. If he chose to he could make things really awkward for her, and she was in enough trouble as it was. As she desperately needed to stay on here at Queen Eleanor's after the exam results came through it was important to have a good record.

Maggie was feeling better and had gone home for the weekend, so when Claire had had something to eat she packed a few of her belongings before getting ready to go out. It was amazing how much junk she seemed to have accumulated since she had been here. It was going to take something the size of a removal van to get all of it over to Wytchend! On the other hand, she didn't see why Steve shouldn't run her over there, after what she was doing for him.

On the dot of four she was ready, dressed in her most demure suit, set off by a trim white shirt and a pair of flat-heeled brogues. As she sat at her dressing table, studying her face, she tried to imagine what the girl most likely to tame Steve Lang would look like, and chuckled as she warmed to the task of adapting herself to the image. Applying the minimum of make-up, she scraped her hair up into a tight, severe knot, then she had a brilliant idea. In her make-up drawer was a pair of glasses she had worn in a play the hospital drama group had put on last year. As a finishing touch she slipped them on and surveyed herself, smiling. That should do it all right. As she rose from the dressing table there was a knock on her door, and she couldn't help feeling a small thrill of anticipation as she went to answer it. She couldn't wait to see Steve's face when he saw her.

He stared disbelievingly at her. 'Good God! What have you done to yourself?'

She blinked at him through the glasses. 'Don't you think I look the part? After all, I'm supposed to be a steadying influence on you, aren't I?'

He shook his head dazedly. 'A steadying influence? Dressed like that you're positively galvanizing! My mother will find it hard to believe I could fall for anyone who looked like that!'

Claire turned with a smile to reach for her neatest bag and gloves. 'Great! She's bound to believe you're a reformed character, then, isn't she?'

All the way to his mother's house a subdued Steve kept glancing sideways at Claire as he drove. She really had gone over the top.

'Couldn't you just take off the specs?' he asked hopefully, but she shook her head.

'There was nothing in our agreement about what I should wear. And you did say you wanted your mother to see me as a sensible girl. But if you don't like it you can take me back right now – don't say I didn't keep the bargain, though.'

He knew when he was beaten. 'Okay,' he sighed. 'Fair enough.'

Mrs Lang was a widow and had recently moved into a delightful house on the outskirts of the town, not so very far from Claire's own home. Steve was her only child and she obviously doted on him, which he clearly found something of a burden. She was waiting for them eagerly at the front door as they parked the car in the drive; a small, blonde woman with a fragile look that belied the indomitable spirit that Steve himself had inherited.

As Claire got out of the car Mrs Lang advanced towards her, hands outstretched, a beaming smile on her face.

'So *this* is the girl my Steve has chosen!' she gushed. 'Ever since he telephoned to tell me the good news I've been so excited!' She gave Claire a kiss on either cheek, then held her at arms' length to scrutinise her carefully.

'Claire, isn't it? What a sweet name. I'm sure you'll be perfect for him. I can see at a glance you're not like all those others – giggling, flighty little things without a thought in their heads. Steve has told me now clever you are and how dedicated. You're going to have such a *fulfilled* life together–' She led them into the house, talking all the time, and the hour that followed was quite the most uncomfortable Claire had ever lived through. She ate postage stamp-sized cucumber sandwiches and fingers of chocolate cake and tried to look adoringly at Steve, though she could cheerfully have strangled him. She needn't have worried about what to say; Mrs Lang never stopped talking herself, going on about Steve and what a perfect child he had been, which, Claire noted with satisfaction, made him squirm uncomfortably on his chair. When at last he announced that it was time to leave, Mrs Lang came out to the drive with them. Leaning in through the window, she kissed Claire fondly.

'Steve has warned me that you won't be able to visit often,' she said, 'so don't worry about it. I quite understand how busy you are, and I shan't worry about him now that I know he has you to keep him out of trouble.'

As Steve turned the car on to the road Claire took off the glasses and slipped them into her bag, turning to glare at him.

'Well, I hope you're satisfied!' she told him. 'I think you're perfectly despicable to deceive your own mother like that – not to mention involving me in your nasty little scheme!'

He looked unrepentant. 'You don't know her,' he said, his eyes flinty. 'Once she gets a bee in her bonnet she never gives me any peace. Desperate ills need desperate remedies.'

Claire sighed, stretching out her legs and leaning her head back luxuriously, relieved that her part in it was over.

'I can understand that she has to be like that, with a son like you,' she told him.

By the time Claire arrived at sixty-two Sycamore Avenue that evening, lugging a large suitcase, she was all in. Her mother looked concerned.

'Darling, why didn't you ring me? I could have come over and picked you up if I'd known you were going to bring all that stuff.'

Claire flopped into a chair. 'It's all right. I got a lift as far as the end of the road,' she said. 'One of the doctors.'

Her mother looked interested. 'Oh yes? How kind.'

Claire sniffed noncommittally. It had been the least Steve could do in the circumstances!

Before changing to nights Claire had three days' break, during which she moved the rest of her belongings back to Sycamore Avenue. Once she had settled snugly back into her old room she and her mother drove down to St Crispin's to bring Mike home for the half-term break. Her mother had made her promise to say nothing to him about her redundancy for the moment, and the three spent a pleasant couple of days together.

It was midweek when Claire reported for duty again, setting out for Kingsmere in her mother's Mini after the family had eaten their evening meal. So far she had not had any response to her advertisement on the notice board, offering lifts in return for sharing expenses. She hoped someone would turn up soon to help out, otherwise her mother would feel obliged to sell the car.

She had just reached the roundabout that led on to the main Kingsmere road when she saw him. He waved a thumb at her, hitch-hiker fashion, and she checked her mirror and pulled over to the side of the road. Steve opened the door and jumped in, throwing her a grateful grin. He wore casual clothes and was obviously going out for the evening.

'Thanks, love,' he said cheerily. 'It seems

your week for being the Good Samaritan, doesn't it?'

She looked at him suspiciously. 'What's wrong with your car? If this is another of your tricks, Steve Lang–'

He shook his head. 'Definitely not guilty, Your Honour. Smashed her up last night – a complete write-off.' He glanced at her. 'It wasn't my fault, actually, though I daresay you'll call it poetic justice.'

'Not if it means my driving you about. I've had enough of you to last for a while,' she told him, negotiating a right turn. 'You may not have heard of them, but there are these big things with six wheels – they're called buses!'

He looked at her. 'If you don't mind my saying so, sweetest, sarcasm doesn't become you. You know, you're getting very hard in your old age. You haven't even asked if I hurt myself!'

Claire snorted. 'No such luck as having you out of action for a few weeks. That would be asking too much of fate!'

He grinned. 'You can't fool me. I know you're only trying not to show how much you love me. Speaking of which, I'm glad to see you looking more yourself this evening.' He turned sideways in his seat to look at her. 'You know, I've been thinking, being engaged to you isn't half a bad idea, not bad at all, when I come to think of it.'

Claire gave a long-suffering sigh. 'I told you, I wouldn't marry you if you were the last man on earth!'

Steve grinned wickedly. 'If I were the last man on earth you'd probably get trampled in the rush! Anyway, I said *engaged*, not married. A fiancée might come in very useful at times.'

She drew up at the kerbside and turned to him. 'I don't know where you're going, but this is as far as I'm taking you,' she said bluntly. 'You can walk the rest of the way. I've really had you up to here, Steve.'

By the time she reached the hospital and parked the car she was still fuming. Steve might be one of Queen Eleanor's brightest housemen, but he was nothing more than a pain as far as she was concerned.

She locked the car carefully and made her way towards Spencer Ward. Visiting hour was just coming to an end and the corridors were full of people, so she didn't notice Simon until he was almost face to face with her. He stopped, standing directly in her path.

'Claire?'

She felt the blood rush into her cheeks. 'Oh, hello.'

'I've been trying to get in touch with you all week,' he said.

'I was swapped back to Spencer, then I went home – time off before changing to nights,' she muttered. 'I've been busy. I've moved out of the Nurses' Home, you see.'

He nodded. 'So I gathered. Well, I suppose it isn't surprising in the circumstances.'

A certain coolness in his tone made her look up at him, and she saw with a small shock that he was angry. The blue eyes flashed like ice and his mouth was set in a straight, tight line. Claire felt indignation rise in her. Did he think she owed him anything because he had bought her dinner the other night? Was she supposed to keep him informed of her every move? How arrogant could he get? And just what did he mean by 'in the circumstances'?

'I have to go,' she said, glancing at her watch. 'I'm on duty in ten minutes.'

'I think your behaviour needs some explanation,' he said, still standing squarely in her way.

Her eyes blazed as she looked up at him. 'I beg your pardon? *My* behaviour? I can't imagine what you mean.'

'Can't you?' He thrust an evening paper into her hands. 'If you really have such a short memory you'll find the answer in there.'

She stared after him as he strode on down the corridor, then down at the newspaper in her hands. Something had made him very angry, but what?

In the kitchen on Spencer Ward the staff nurse who was going off duty smiled at her. 'Good evening, Nurse Simms. I believe congratulations are in order.'

Claire looked puzzled. 'Oh – er – are they?'

As she bustled from the room Claire glanced at a first-year nurse who was washing up cups and saucers. 'Have you any idea what she means?'

Nurse Graham shrugged. 'Sorry.'

Claire opened the evening paper that Simon had pushed at her and spread it out on the worktop, turning the pages and looking at each one carefully. She couldn't see anything that could be remotely connected with her. Then it caught her eye, there in the announcements column: *Engagements. Lang – Simms: Mrs Valerie Lang is delighted to announce the engagement of her only son, Steven John, to Miss Claire Simms.*

Claire gasped. This time Steve had really landed her in it! She wondered furiously if he had known about the announcement when he had thumbed a lift from her earlier. With all her heart she longed to tell him what she thought of him, ached to slap his silly self-satisfied face–

'Nurse Simms! Are we to have the pleasure of your company on the ward to-night, or do you find that newspaper more interesting than the patients?' It was Sister Grey, who had just come on duty, standing framed in the doorway like the angel of doom. Hurriedly Claire bundled the paper out of sight.

'Sorry, Sister.' She straightened her cap in the mirror over the sink and walked out into the corridor, where Sister turned to survey her frostily.

'A word of advice while we're alone, Nurse. I feel it's bad policy to become too arrogant simply because one is engaged to one of the doctors on the staff. It's a very bad example to an impressionable young first-year nurse like Graham.'

Claire opened her mouth to protest, then shut it again as Sister walked away, apron rustling with righteous indignation. What was the use of denying something they had all seen printed in black and white? This was something she would find very difficult to explain away – very difficult indeed!

CHAPTER FIVE

As far as the ward was concerned it was a quiet night. Claire found that Peter Johnson, the young diabetic, was still there, due to be discharged tomorrow. He was unable to sleep, and at two in the morning she made him a cup of tea. She was still in the ward kitchen when someone tapped on the door and came in, and turning, she caught her breath with surprise when she saw that it was Simon.

'Oh, hello. I've just made some tea, would you like a cup? It's still hot.' Apprehension made her fumble, clattering the crockery clumsily as she reached for another cup from the cupboard.

'No, please don't trouble,' he said quickly. 'I just came up to tell you that your friend Miss Grainger is being discharged tomorrow. She's been asking for you.'

Claire nodded. 'Of course, she'll be wanting George back. I'll take him over tomorrow when I'm off duty.' They stood looking at each other for a moment, then she took a deep breath and said: 'About what you saw in the paper, about Steve and me–'

He shook his head, frowning. 'You needn't worry, I shan't say anything to your – fiancée about the other evening.'

His stiffness of tone annoyed her. 'There's nothing to tell, is there?' she retorted indignantly. 'Except that you asked me to have dinner with you because someone else had let you down!'

Simon put a hand into his pocket. 'By the way, I meant to give you this. I found it next morning on the floor in my living room.' He took out a handkerchief and she snatched it from him, her face flushing warmly.

'I'm surprised you bothered to return it,' she told him, her voice tart with humiliation. 'I'd have imagined you'd keep it to put with the rest of your – *trophies!* By the way, I forgot to tell you that your friend Sally rang the other night while you were getting the milk. She wanted you to ring her back.'

His eyes widened as he stared at her. 'Sally?' he echoed, the colour leaving his face. Just for a moment Claire knew a spurt of triumphant satisfaction. So now he knew that she'd seen through his little game! His eyes narrowed as they fixed on her face, waiting for her to expand on her remark, and suddenly her nerve was gone. Her mouth dried and she wanted with all her heart to take back her acid remarks, though she didn't quite know why. Quite clearly the mention of the name Sally had shocked him. It was all so silly, this game they were playing; why couldn't she have pocketed her pride and explained the fiasco about her alleged 'engagement' at once, asked him for an explanation about Sally too – brought everything out in the open? But now it was clearly too late. Without another word Simon, his face grim, turned on his heel and left. Claire stood, frozen with anguish, biting her lip as she listened to his footsteps going down the corridor, then she closed the door and leaned against it, eyes closed and fists clenched as she cursed her own stubbornness and the luck that fate seemed determined to deal her.

When she emerged into the outside world next morning she breathed in the fresh air gratefully. The sun was shining and at last there was a hint of spring in the air, but Claire hardly noticed as she faced the drive out to Wytchend. It was at times like this that she would miss the close proximity of her room in the Nurses' Home, where she could slip out of her clothes and be asleep within minutes of coming off duty if she felt like it. This morning she felt more than usually weary, and put it down to emotional strain. For most of the small hours she had agonised about her encounter with Simon. Why had her stupid pride forbidden her to tell him the truth of the matter, however bizarre it might have sounded? It would have been better than letting him think that her conscience was as adaptable as his!

She thought about the girl in the photograph, remembering the beautiful face and the loving message she had written, and her conscience did an about-face. To think that he had accused *her* of disloyalty! Simon Bonham wasn't worth all the disruption he was causing her!

Although she missed her room at the Nurses' Home it was nice to have her breakfast waiting when she got home. As she ate it her mother placed the evening paper on the table between them, open at the announcements page, an enquiring expression on her face. Claire sighed.

'Oh dear, you too?' As briefly as she could she explained the muddle, and Rosemary shook her head.

'You're too soft, Claire. One of these days

it will get you into trouble.'

Claire nodded. Hadn't it already?

Soon afterwards her mother packed her off to bed, where she slept soundly until three o'clock. Later, as she sat finishing her meal, she looked at her young brother.

'Like to help me with something this afternoon, Mike?'

He looked up eagerly. 'Yes, what is it?'

She nodded towards the cage where the budgie chattered happily. 'I have to take George back to his owner this afternoon – she came out of hospital this morning. I'm sure she'd like to meet you, and you might be able to make yourself useful – do a bit of shopping for her.'

Her mother looked up. 'That's a good idea. I daresay the poor old soul will be feeling lonely after the company in hospital. I'll tell you what – I'll make a sponge cake for you to take her.'

Miss Grainger was delighted to see them and overjoyed to have George back. Mike was despatched to the corner shop with a shopping list and Claire helped Miss Grainger to make tea, ready for his return..

On the way home in her car Mike looked at her with a mixture of curiosity and admiration. 'Do you do that kind of thing for all your patients?'

Claire laughed. 'Good heavens, no! I'd never have any time to myself if I did. In fact I got into hot water for getting too involved with Miss Grainger.'

He looked at her. 'Why did you? I mean, what was special about her?'

Claire sighed. 'She didn't have anyone – anyone at all, and suddenly it made me see how lucky I was to be part of a family.' She turned to smile at him. 'You may be a little horror, but you are my brother.'

He grinned. 'I know what you mean.' Then his face clouded. 'Claire, why hasn't Mum been to work this week?'

She glanced at him. 'I suppose she took time off to be with you for the half-term break.'

He shook his head. 'I don't think so, somehow. She tries to hide it, but I think there's something worrying her.'

'What makes you say that?'

Mike sighed. 'The other night I woke up and came down for something to eat, and she was in the living room, in her dressing gown – at two in the morning.'

Claire tried to shrug it off. 'You know how she loves to watch the late night film. Maybe she nodded off to sleep.'

'No, she hadn't been watching television. She was sitting at the table – with bank-books and other things. She was using a calculator – the one you bought her for Christmas. I think she was trying to work something out. I asked if I could help, but she got a bit agitated – bundled everything away before I could see it.'

She swallowed hard. 'Mum does have a life of her own, you know, Mike,' she said. 'I wouldn't press her if I were you.'

But he looked unconvinced. 'Maybe it was something to do with that letter I brought home with me,' he said thoughtfully.

'Letter – what letter?' Claire looked at him sharply.

'It was from the Head,' Mike told her. 'We all had one.'

It was another two days before Claire got the chance to ask her mother about the letter. She had to wait until Mike had gone back to school. She had just got home and was sitting at the kitchen table while her mother boiled eggs for breakfast.

'Mum, you didn't tell me you had a letter from Mike's Headmaster,' she said. 'What was it about?'

It was several seconds before her mother turned round, and when she did Claire saw that she was desperately worried. She spooned the eggs into their cups, avoiding her daughter's searching eyes, then sat down in the chair opposite, her shoulders slumped despairingly.

'I hoped you wouldn't get to know,' she sighed. 'You're already trying to help – working so hard.' She glanced up. 'But I suppose you'll have to know soon anyway. Mike's school fees have gone up.' She gave a long sigh as though telling Claire was a relief. 'It really couldn't have come at a worse time,' she went on. 'I sat up nearly all one night trying to work out our finances, but it's no use. We're going to have to sell the house.'

Claire sighed. 'Oh dear, I thought it might be something like that. Look, Mum, I'm sure if Mike knew he'd be willing to change to another school. He'd hate to see you going without – pinching and saving all for him.'

But Rosemary Simms was not to be moved. 'No. It was what your father wanted. He was so proud on the day that Mike passed the entrance exam for St Crispin's. I couldn't let his memory down like that – or Mike either. It's better if we sell the house, that way you won't have to make sacrifices.'

'But what about *you*, Mum?' Claire could have shaken her mother at that moment. 'By the time Mike's education is complete you'll have no money left, and he wouldn't want that! Do you want him to feel guilty for the rest of his life?'

'He need never know,' Rosemary said firmly, looking at her daughter as if defying her to betray her secret. 'He never *will* know if I have anything to do with it.'

'Promise me one thing,' said Claire, looking at her mother. 'Don't do anything yet. You might land one of the jobs you've applied for – something might turn up. Don't do anything impulsive.' Already a plan was forming in her own mind, but she intended to keep quiet about it for the moment.

It was on her way to the hospital the following evening that she began to put the plan into action. Most evenings she stopped for petrol at a garage just off the bypass, and she had become quite friendly with the owner, a smiling, middle-aged man who had been a patient at Queen Eleanor's in Claire's second year. Only a few days ago he had told her that the boy who served part-time on the pumps had left to join the Army, leaving him shorthanded. This evening she got out of the car as he slipped the hose into the Mini's petrol tank.

'Mr Palmer–' she began hesitantly.

He looked up with a smile. 'Yes, Nurse?'

She cleared her throat. 'You said the other night that you were short-staffed. I – er – wondered if I could help?'

He withdrew the hose and clipped it back on to the side of the pump, looking at her with a puzzled expression. 'Help? I don't see how.'

'I mean serving petrol,' she told him. 'Of course I'd have to fit the hours in with my shifts, but I was thinking – it would often fit in with your busiest times.' She looked at him hopefully. 'What do you say?'

Mr Palmer pushed the baseball cap he always wore to the back of his head and surveyed her thoughtfully. 'I do believe you're serious,' he said.

She nodded. 'I am! Please, will you give it some thought, Mr Palmer? I'd be very grateful.'

He looked doubtful. 'I don't know. What about those pretty hands of yours? Can't have a nurse with oil under her fingernails.'

'I'd wear gloves,' she assured him. 'I've thought of all that, honestly.' She looked at him with appealing grey eyes. 'I really do need the extra money, Mr Palmer.'

He smiled. 'All right then, you're on. Let's say a week's trial – either way. Start on Monday – all right?'

She smiled. 'Monday I'll be on days, so I could work here in the evenings.'

'Suits me,' he told her. 'Six till ten. I'll pay you the same as I paid the lad. Okay?'

Claire climbed back into the car and gave him a wave. 'Great! See you then, Mr Palmer.'

The first two weeks of her 'moonlighting' job were hard for Claire, and when she crawled into bed at night she was almost too tired to sleep. Her mother worried about her.

'I wish you'd simply agree to my selling the house,' she complained.

'I'll be fine when I get into my stride, just give me time,' Claire assured her, though she had carefully avoided telling her mother just what her job entailed, leaving her under the impression that she was acting as cashier at the garage – not serving at the pumps.

At last the 'flu epidemic seemed to be over, and one afternoon during visiting time she was in the kitchen, making a pot of tea for Sister, when Steve's head came round the door.

'Hi there! I haven't had a chance to see you on your own lately. How have you been?'

Claire groaned at the sight of him. 'Oh, it's you. What do you want now? I'm still trying to live down the last fix you got me into. By the time I'd been round everyone telling them it was all a silly practical joke I was almost hoarse, not to mention sick and tired of the very thought of you!'

He sighed. 'Sorry about that. I wasn't to know my mother'd go and put that notice in the paper without telling me first, was I?'

She turned away to lay Sister's tray. 'I wouldn't put it past you. I wouldn't put *anything* past you!'

He laid a hand on her arm. 'Ah, now is that kind? Look, let me make it up to you. Let me take you for a spin in my new car this evening.'

She shook her head. 'Can't.'

Steve frowned. 'What do you mean, can't?'

She turned to him angrily, her eyes flashing. 'Even you can understand English, Steve. I mean exactly what I said: I can't. I'm busy.'

'Doing what?' he persisted, standing in her way. 'Going out with Bonham, I'll bet!'

She rounded on him. 'Any chance of that was polished off by you! Now will you please get out of my way? Sister's waiting for this tea.'

He stood firm. 'Not till you explain that last remark and tell me where you're going.'

Claire picked up the tray and moved towards the door, but he stepped sideways, blocking it. It was unfortunate that Sister chose that very moment to come into the kitchen. She pushed the door, hitting Steve in the back, and he stumbled forward, knocking the tray from Claire's hands. There was a crash as teapot, cups and saucers scattered in a mess of spilled tea and broken china on the floor. Claire stared at it, then to her own horror and the astonishment of Sister and Steve Lang, she burst into tears.

'What on *earth*-?' Sister stared at the mess, then at Claire, turning a steely eye on Steve. 'Dr Lang, I really cannot have you up here upsetting my nurses,' she admonished. 'I've had occasion to complain about you before, and I certainly shan't hesitate to do so again if you persist in disrupting my ward like this!' She looked at Claire, who was on her knees clearing up the mess on the floor, grateful to have something to do while she fought for control.

'You'd better take your tea break now,

Nurse Simms. Take ten minutes extra and try to compose yourself. And before you go off duty I should like to see you in my office.'

In the canteen Claire sipped the hot cup of tea bought for her by a penitent Steve. While she drank it he stared helplessly at her white face.

'Honestly, love, I'm sorry. I do seem to bring you rather a lot of bad luck, don't I? I don't mean to, you know.' When she didn't answer he leaned forward. 'Look, I'm not as insensitive as all that. I can see that something's wrong. Won't you tell me what it is?'

She hesitated. She longed to pour out her troubles to someone, but Steve was not the person. He might not mean to, but he had a positive talent for turning her life upside down. After the Paracetamol incident she felt that the less he knew about her private life, the better.

'It's just the travelling since I went home to live,' she told him. 'I find it tires me out.'

He looked sympathetic. 'Poor old sausage! Can't you and your mother move nearer?'

'Oh, I'll get used to it,' she assured him. 'And now I'd better get back to the ward and try to get back into Sister's good books!'

The interview with Sister wasn't as bad as she had feared.

'Would you like to tell me what the trouble is?' she asked as soon as Claire was seated.

Claire had decided to tell Sister the same story as she had told Steve.

'I'm afraid the extra travelling makes me tired – but I shall get used to it, I'm sure,' she added hurriedly.

Sister looked closely at her. 'You're sure there's nothing else – nothing to do with Dr Lang? I've heard various stories–'

Claire sighed. 'There's absolutely no truth in them. I'm afraid some of his practical jokes go a bit too far at times.'

Sister looked thoughtful. 'Well, I daresay this has been a hard winter for us all, but more so for you, with your finals and everything. You'll be better when your results come through, I daresay.' She smiled at Claire somewhat frostily. 'But do try to get more rest. Tired, irritable nurses are no use on this ward or any other!' She rose from her desk. 'Off you go now and have a nice relaxing evening.'

Claire groaned inwardly. What a hope!

It was as she was coming out of Mr Palmer's office that evening after changing into the overalls she wore for the job that she had her first shock. A car was just drawing on to the forecourt and at the wheel sat Mr Jamieson, the Hospital Administrator. Claire turned and disappeared back into the office. Muttering an excuse, she fumbled with one of her shoes while Mr Palmer went out to serve Mr Jamieson himself. It was a narrow escape. Somehow she had never thought of having to serve anyone from the hospital. Palmer's garage was off the bypass and as far as she knew not many of the hospital staff used it. While he was serving Claire looked round Mr Palmer's office. Hanging on a hook behind the door she found another baseball cap and, standing in front of the cracked mirror, she pulled it on, tucking all her hair up underneath it. It was just what she needed, the peak would hide her face if she pulled it well over her eyes and kept her head down. Feeling a little more secure, she walked out on to the forecourt.

'If you want to go for a break I'm ready to take over now,' she told the garage owner.

He took in her 'disguise' and hid a smile. 'Good. As a matter of fact, Claire, I was wondering if I could leave you in charge this evening – I have a meeting to attend. I'll take the day's takings home with me and I know I can trust you to put whatever else you take into the safe and lock up. Do you mind?'

'Of course not,' she assured him.

She busied herself doing the chores she always did in between customers. It was a pleasant evening and she was just reflecting that it would be nice to be going for a drive herself when she heard another car drive on to the forecourt. She turned – and got the shock of her life when she found herself looking at Simon Bonham's sleek silver-grey Alfa Romeo. Simon sat at the wheel and, next to him, Dr Gillian Blair, the glamorous new addition to Mr Fairbrother's firm.

With a dry mouth and burning cheeks, Claire walked on to the forecourt and waited for instructions. Simon wound down his window and asked for four gallons, and the minutes ticked by slowly as she waited for the pump to discharge petrol into the Alfa Romeo's tank, her head averted. Never had she known four gallons to take so long! She pulled the peak of the baseball cap a little further over her eyes as she leaned forward for the money. His hand came out of the window, offering exactly the right amount, and she took it gratefully, muttering gruff thanks. As the car pulled away on to the road she drew a long breath of relief. If Simon had recognised her he had given no sign of it. Had the overalls and the cap fooled him into taking her for the boy who used to serve here? As she stood watching the car disappear from view she wondered wistfully where he was going with Dr Blair, and felt a sharp little pang of jealousy. Everyone had been talking about the attractive and brilliant young woman doctor since her arrival at Queen Eleanor's a few weeks ago. Simon would have more in common with her than with a third-year nurse. No doubt he had her lined up as Sally's next rival, Claire told herself bitterly as she worked. She only hoped he would take a little more trouble in hiding the photograph this time!

Around nine-thirty there was a lull, and Claire looked at her watch, wondering if she should close the garage a little early. She was sure Mr Palmer wouldn't mind as she was on her own, and she could certainly do with an early night.

She went into the office and switched off the forecourt lights. Opening the till, she counted the money. It was surprising how much she had taken in just a few hours. Although Mr Palmer had taken the day's takings away with him there was still over two hundred pounds to put into the safe. She counted it carefully into the cashbox, too occupied to notice the battered van that drew up outside. Its occupant, a youth, dressed in jeans, an anorak and trainers, got out and came silently into the shop, and Claire looked up, startled, as he spoke.

'All right, darlin', just hand it over here and you won't get hurt.' The words were mild enough, but the steely way they were delivered struck terror into Claire's heart. One read of this kind of thing happening but never imagined it taking place in real life, somehow. Thoughts sped through her mind as she stared into the hard young eyes. Why had she never asked whether Mr Palmer had a burglar alarm? Could she reach the telephone, or make a dash for the door? Was that bulge under the intruder's anorak a weapon of some sort?

As though he read her thoughts and without taking the cold eyes off her, the youth kicked the door shut behind him.

'You heard me,' he said, his voice becoming louder. 'Hand it over – *now*. If not–' He slipped one hand threateningly inside the anorak and Claire's heart thudded with apprehension. Then, out of the corner of her eye, she caught sight of a car, edging its way smoothly and silently on to the forecourt. With the door closed and his back to it, the youth neither saw nor heard its arrival.

'I – I'm not alone here,' said Claire, stalling for time. 'My boss is out at the back. I only have to call–'

He laughed nastily. 'I've been watching all evening,' he told her. 'He's gone for the night, so don't try to fool me.' He took a step nearer. 'Now, hand it over. Why should you care? It's no skin off your nose, is it?'

She tried hard not to draw the youth's attention to the car outside, but out of the corner of her eye she had seen someone get out of it. A shadowy figure was walking stealthily towards the shop. With the lights out she had no way of seeing who it was. Then a chilling thought struck her: it might be an accomplice! She would stand no chance against two of them – no chance at all! Her heart was beating very fast as she waited helplessly, then suddenly it almost stopped as the door was flung open, striking the youth and knocking him off balance.

In a state of petrified shock, Claire watched the struggle that ensued. For a moment all was confusion, the two men a blur of flailing arms and legs, but the youth was slight in build and was soon over-powered by the heavier man, reduced to a white-faced, quivering wreck, while Claire hurriedly dialled 999 with trembling fingers, wondering dazedly how on earth Simon Bonham came to be passing this way for a second time in one evening and what had prompted him to call in.

It was another hour before they could leave Palmer's garage, having given a state-ment to the police and waited until a shocked Mr Palmer arrived. Simon took charge, his face stony as he ordered Claire:

'Get changed. I'm taking you home – you're in no state to drive.' He turned to Mr Palmer. 'Perhaps you can arrange for Miss Simms' Mini to be delivered to her home. I very much doubt whether she'll be working here any more after tonight.'

Claire stared at him. How dared he speak for her? 'Oh, but I must–' she began, but Simon silenced her with a look.

Mr Palmer was apologetic. 'I wouldn't have had this happen for the world,' he told her. 'I'll call round tomorrow to see how you are. I should never have left you to cope on your own – I might have known–'

'Yes, you might! If you want my opinion, I think it was criminal to leave a defenceless young woman in charge.' Simon's face was stern as he took Claire by the arm. 'If you're ready, we'll go.'

In the car Claire sat in silence. Of course she was grateful to Simon. If he hadn't arrived when he had she might have been hurt – the policeman had discovered a sawn-off shotgun inside the youth's anorak. But at the same time she was indignant at the way he had spoken to Mr Palmer, refusing to allow her to speak for herself. Suddenly she thought of her mother; if she should hear about what had happened it would only add to her worries. She turned to Simon.

'I'm grateful to you for taking me home,' she said quietly. 'If you just drop me off at the end of the road–'

Without a word he pulled over and stopped the car, turning to her.

'I'm still waiting for an explanation,' he told her abruptly.

She looked at him. 'The garage was almost robbed,' she began foolishly, and an expression of irritation crossed his face.

'I gathered that,' he said dryly. 'I'm not in the habit of tackling innocent customers. I want to hear your part in all this. What were you doing, dressed up in that ridiculous fancy dress and serving petrol?'

Claire bit her lip, her eyes unable to meet his. 'I told you – I'm grateful to you for coming to my rescue, but I really don't see that it's any of your business.'

'I happen to think it is,' he insisted. 'Don't you think that as a nurse you owe it to your patients to reserve your energy?'

'Oh, don't be so damned *pompous!*' The events of the past hour had frayed her nerves to snapping point and the moment the words were out she felt the tears rise in her throat, almost choking her. What did *he* know? Sitting there, calmly telling her what she should do! His life was a piece of cake compared to hers! She struggled desperately for control, biting her lips hard.

Silently he handed her a large, clean handkerchief. 'Here, have a good cry if you feel like it. I don't mind.' he looked at her thoughtfully for a moment. 'I suppose the idea of moonlighting was to save up for your trousseau.'

She stared at him, ignoring the proffered hanky. 'I thought I'd squashed *that* rumour once and for all.'

'A public announcement can hardly be termed a rumour,' he told her crisply.

'If you knew Steve Lang as I do you'd

know that anything he's mixed up in very soon becomes complicated almost beyond belief,' she told him wearily. 'Any girl who agreed to marry him would need her head testing!' She turned to look at him. 'Let's just say that I owed him a favour and for reasons best known to himself he needed someone to play the part of his fiancée for one afternoon.' She shrugged. 'Things got hopelessly out of hand. I should have known they would.' She stole a glance at Simon and saw that his grim expression had lightened a little.

'I see.' He turned to look at her. 'It still seems pretty irresponsible to me, but it still doesn't explain why you were working at the garage.'

Claire looked at her watch, her nerves jangling. By now her mother would be wondering where she was. 'My private problems are my own business – whatever you think,' she told him. 'I'm grateful for what you did tonight, but that doesn't entitle you to *interrogate* me! I just wish you'd stop trying to interfere in my life.' She glanced at him out of the corner of her eye, itching to wipe that calm, superior expression from his handsome face. 'Why don't you concentrate on Dr Blair?' she lashed. 'She's more your type, surely?' He was silent and she bit her lip hard. Why on earth had she said that? She took a deep breath. 'If you don't mind I'd rather like to go home now,' she said miserably.

Without a word Simon started the car and drove on. As he stopped outside the house in Sycamore Avenue Claire opened the door, scanning the windows for her mother's anxious face. She began to get out, but he stopped her, a hand on her arm.

'Claire, wait. What are you going to tell your mother? You're upset, and – I hesitate to say this, but it shows.'

In the heat of the moment she hadn't even thought about this, and she checked, turning, half in and out of the car, to stare at him in dismay. 'Oh God! I don't know. I can't tell her what really happened – she'd be so horrified. She thinks I was cashier at Palmer's. I told her that because she was worried already–' She broke off helplessly and he touched her shoulder.

'Look, to save you getting yourself embroiled in any more problems, you'd better let me come in with you and help. We can say that you felt unwell and I happened to call in for petrol and offered you a lift home. You need a reason for not going back to

Palmer's too, don't you?'

Her nerves were as taut as violin strings as she looked up at him. She had just told him to stop interfering, but now she had to admit that she needed his help. There was no other way. A feeling of despair washed over her as the full implications of the night's happening struck home.

'It won't get into the papers, will it?' she asked in a whisper. 'Heaven knows what they'd make of it at Queen Eleanor's if it does!' She looked up at him, her eyes widening. 'I've involved you too. Oh Lord, I'm sorry.' The tears that she had successfully swallowed earlier welled up now, trickling helplessly down her cheeks as she fumbled for a hanky. 'Oh, what a mess!' she sniffed.

Simon reached out an arm, encircling her shoulders to draw her gently against his shoulder.

'Don't worry about the papers,' he said reassuringly. 'You can leave that with me.' He gave her shoulders a comforting squeeze. 'Go on, let out all that tension – you'll feel better for it. After that I'm coming in with you, just to see that we both have the same story. There's no other way, Claire. I promise you it'll be just this once. After tonight I won't interfere in your life ever again, you can rely on it.'

When she heard her daughter's key in the lock Rosemary Simms came out into the hall. 'Claire, thank goodness you're home! I was beginning to wonder–' She broke off as she saw that Claire wasn't alone. 'Oh, I'm sorry–'

'This is Dr Bonham, Mum. He brought me home,' Claire explained. Simon stepped forward and offered Rosemary his hand.

'I stopped at Palmer's for petrol and Claire wasn't feeling very well, so I thought I'd better see her safely home,' he said, smiling.

Rosemary looked anxiously at Claire. 'Oh dear, I knew you'd overdo it, working all those hours and on your feet all day too. Off you go to bed and I'll bring you a hot drink.' She looked apologetically at Simon. 'You'll stay and have one too, won't you, Doctor? It's the least I can do.'

He opened his mouth to refuse, then saw the look of silent appeal on Rosemary's face. There was something vulnerable and helpless about the woman. Perhaps there was more to Claire's problems than he had thought. He smiled his assent.

'Thank you, that would be very nice.'

Tucked up in bed, Claire sipped at the hot

chocolate her mother had brought her, toasting her toes on the comforting hot water bottle. What a day! Surely things must have reached rock bottom. There was only one consolation: the Simms family fortunes could surely only go one way now, and that was up! Downstairs she could still hear the rumble of conversation, her mother's light voice, interspersed with Simon's deep one, and the sound made her slightly uneasy. What could they possibly be finding to talk about all this time? Simon had promised not to mention the hold-up to her mother. Surely he wouldn't let her down on that? She thought about the conversation they had had in the car, her heart sinking. Why had she said such stupid things? She put the empty cup on the bedside table and slid down under the covers, exhaustion making her head spin and her eyelids heavy, but as sleep engulfed her Simon's words echoed in her head:

'Just this once, Claire. I promise you that after that I won't interfere in your life ever again. You can rely on it.'

Quite clearly she had put an end to any relationship they might have had. He could hardly have told her more plainly. She couldn't say she blamed him either! Curled up in the warmth of her bed she fought to stay awake a little longer, to unravel the threads of thought tangling in her mind, but it was no use; the day had been too full of happenings. Sleep drew its curtain at last. The last sound she was conscious of was Simon's voice downstairs. It was strangely comforting.

CHAPTER SIX

Claire had been right about the Simms'
family fortunes not being able to fall any
lower. From the evening of the hold-up at
Palmer's garage life began to look more
hopeful. No more disasters occurred, winter
suddenly blossomed into spring and,
physically, Claire felt better almost at once
when she had given up her evening job at
the garage. Apart from showing concern
about her health Rosemary had said little
about the events of that evening, much to
Claire's relief. When she had probed gently
to try to find out what Simon and her
mother had talked about over their chocolate after she had gone to bed that night,
Rosemary had simply remarked that he was
one of the nicest, most sympathetic doctors
she had ever met and that she was glad that
Claire had had the good sense to take his
advice about giving up her moonlighting.

It was as she was coming home one
mellow evening about three weeks later that
the first sign of their change in fortune

manifested itself. She saw the board as soon as she turned the corner of the road. It stood out conspicuously, a large red and white 'For Sale' notice planted among the newly budding shrubs in the neat front gardens. From this distance she couldn't see just which house it belonged to and she wondered vaguely who could be moving, then as she drew nearer she saw with a small shock that it stood in the Simms' front garden. The moment she got indoors she rushed through to the kitchen to find her mother.

'Mum! There's a "For Sale" notice in the front garden!'

Rosemary turned to look at her, a smile on her lips. 'I know, dear. The agents put it there this morning, and would you believe it, I've already had an offer – a good one!'

Claire shook her head, feeling slightly dazed. 'But I don't understand. Why? You didn't say anything to me. Shouldn't we have discussed it?'

Rosemary sat down at the kitchen table. 'Forgive me for taking matters into my own hands, darling, but knowing how you felt I guessed you would only have talked me out of it again. I've given the matter a lot of thought lately and I'm sure this is the right thing to do. It really isn't sensible, you know, living so far out of town, and the garden really is too much for us to manage now that we're on our own. I heard about this flat, really close to the hospital, and I made up my mind to take the plunge. It's very spacious. I know you'll like it. There's plenty of room for all three of us – and after all, one of these days you'll want to leave and have a place of your own. Besides–'

'*Hey*, steady – wait for me!' protested Claire, laughing. 'Do you think we might take this slowly, one bit at a time? How did you hear about the flat? And when did you make this momentous decision?' She was looking at her mother with new eyes. How was it that she had suddenly become so well adjusted to her widowhood and able to make important decisions all on her own? She sat down opposite. 'Now look – you're not doing all this just for me, are you?'

Rosemary shook her head firmly. 'No. There's another reason.'

Claire waited, but when no further information was offered she said edgily: 'Oh, Mum, don't be so maddening. *Tell* me!'

Rosemary sighed. 'I was saving it as a surprise – if it comes to anything, that is. I don't even know if it will yet.'

'If *what* will come to anything? Mum, if you don't come clean this minute I swear I'll scream!'

Her mother took a deep breath. 'I think there's a good chance I might have got myself another job,' she said in a rush. 'There, now you know.'

Claire stared at her. 'That's something else you never breathed a word about! You mean you applied, without even telling me?'

Rosemary looked slightly shamefaced. 'I'm sure you'll approve,' she said, holding up crossed fingers. '*If* I get it.'

'Well, where is it – and what?' asked Claire.

'That's the marvellous part. It's at the hospital,' her mother told her. 'Personal secretary to Dr Phillips, the diabetic consultant!'

Claire tried to hide her doubt. All the consultants' secretaries at the hospital were young. There was no rule about it, of course, it just seemed to be that way. 'Well, when is the interview?' she asked. 'When do you expect to hear if you're on the short list?'

'The interview was this morning!' Rosemary couldn't quite keep the triumph out of her voice or the sparkle from her eyes as they met Claire's startled ones. Suddenly she burst out laughing. 'Darling, if only you could see your face! Anyone would think I was completely incapable of doing anything by myself. I did hold down a good job with a solicitor, you know.'

'Of course. I didn't – it's all so sudden and unexpected, that's all,' Claire stammered.

'I kept thinking all the time I was at the hospital that I might run into you,' said Rosemary. 'I was there most of the morning. And then when I got home the phone was ringing and these people wanted to come and view the house.' She reached across the table to take Claire's hands, her eyes shining. 'Oh, Claire, they're such a sweet young couple. They need another bedroom because they're expecting their first baby. And they've already sold their house, so there shouldn't be any hold-up over the sale. They fell in love with this place right away.' She clasped her hands together in delight. 'You know, I really believe our luck has taken a turn for the better!'

'Now wait,' Claire said cautiously. 'You can't rely on first impressions, you know. Those people could change their minds. They might see something even more suitable. And it isn't certain you'll get the job. Then there's this flat – by the time we know whether we've sold the house it might have been let.'

But Rosemary refused to be put off. 'What a pessimist you are!' she laughed. 'Just like your father used to be when I got excited about anything. The flat won't go. It's for sale and the owner has promised me first refusal. I've already phoned to let him know provisionally that we'll have it. With what we get for this we'll have enough over to put a nice little nest-egg in the bank! And you're wrong about that couple – I'm sure they won't change their minds.'

'And the job?' asked Claire. 'Are you as confident about that?'

Rosemary's mouth lifted at the corners in a little smile that Claire could only describe as coy. 'I think I made a reasonably good impression,' she said. 'We'll just have to wait and see, won't we?'

She proved to be right in her optimism. The agent telephoned the following morn-ing to confirm that the couple who had viewed the house were definitely going ahead with the purchase. Claire was on a late shift and took the call herself. Later, during doctor's rounds on Spencer Ward, she saw Dr Phillips smiling benignly at her, and before he left he drew her to one side.

'I expect you know that I interviewed your mother for the post of secretary yesterday?' he said confidentially.

Claire nodded. 'Yes, sir, she was telling me.' She looked up at him, wondering if he was going to ask her to let her mother down lightly, but he went on, smiling reminiscently.

'A charming woman – delightful personality, and so efficient. Glowing references, and her typing is immaculate. I daresay I shouldn't say this to you, but so many of the young girls just can't spell nowadays.' He shook his head. 'A sad reflection on our educational system, I'm afraid.'

Claire was staring at him in surprise. She had hardly expected her mother to make such an impression on the usually rather dour consultant. 'I know she enjoyed her interview,' she said.

He cleared his throat, trying not to look flattered. 'Did she really? Good – I'm so glad.' He patted her shoulder, bending to speak quietly into her ear. 'I daresay she'll have some news for you later today.' He tapped the side of his nose. 'Off the record, of course – all to be confirmed through the official channels.'

She watched him walk away from her

down the ward; a tall distinguished man with thick grey hair and perceptive blue eyes. Funny, he was almost handsome when he smiled. She didn't remember seeing him in such a good mood. There was quite a spring in his step this morning, and she felt her own heart lift in response. Perhaps her mother had been right in her hunch about their luck changing after all.

After that things moved fast. Rosemary started her new job the following Monday and the couple who had bought the house announced that they wanted to move in as soon as they could. It seemed that their own buyer was anxious to take possession. The weeks that followed were a mad whirl of packing, planning and organising, culminating in their final removal one lovely spring morning just a month later. Dr Phillips had given Rosemary the day off for the move and Claire was taking her break between day and night shifts.

When the removal men had gone, leaving them standing among a sea of packing cases, Claire looked around her appreciatively. The flat really was a find, overlooking the wooded country that surrounded the hospital. When they were straight she was sure they were going to be comfortable here. She glanced across at her mother, who was busy looking for the kettle.

'You're sure you're going to like it here, Mum?' she asked. 'You won't miss the garden – all the things you and Dad made?'

Rosemary straightened up, her face flushed with triumph as she held up the missing kettle. 'Here it is! Whatever made me pack it in the blanket chest? Now we can have that coffee – I'm gasping!'

Claire followed her into the neat kitchen, repeating her question, and Rosemary turned from the sink, her face thoughtful as she sank into a chair.

'I've been taking stock of my life over the past few weeks, dear,' she said quietly. 'When something happens to change everything you can do two things – live in the past for the rest of your life or make a new start. I decided to make a new start. Better to do it in new surroundings – quite apart from the convenience of all this.' She swept her arm out to embrace the new flat, then smiled gently into Claire's pensive eyes. 'It doesn't mean I'm trying to forget your father; just that I have to learn to live without him, and while everything around me is what we shared I can't do that. Maybe for some women it's comforting, but it doesn't work like that for me. Realising that was what changed everything. Everything seems so much simpler now.'

Claire swallowed the lump in her throat. She had never known her mother possessed such courage. She managed a smile.

'I'm sure you're right.' She stood up to switch off the steaming kettle. 'I'll make the coffee, shall I? Then we'd better start on the unpacking.'

Rosemary turned to look at her. 'While we're on the subject, I want you to know how much I appreciate having a daughter like you,' she said. 'All that you did when we were so desperate for money. But now we have money in the bank, I have a good job and soon you'll be fully qualified. It's all been worth it; But make no mistake, I know that none of it could have happened without you.'

'Rubbish, I hardly did anything,' Claire protested as she passed a mug of coffee to her mother. 'Are you really sure you like working for Dr Phillips? If you're finding it hard I daresay we could manage without your money soon.'

Her mother shook her head. 'I wouldn't think of leaving.' She cupped her hands round, the mug, looking down into it. 'I'll admit that I found it all rather strange at first – all those medical terms and the names of illnesses, treatments and so on. But David Phillips has been so patient and kind, it's a pleasure to work for him. I really look forward to going in each day.' And Claire saw by the look on her face that she meant every word. In fact, since their luck had changed her mother looked ten years younger. She'd had her hair done in a new, younger style and took meticulous care over her appearance each morning before setting off for work.

For one very good reason Claire was glad that life had been hectic over the past weeks. Simon had been true to his word, and apart from their inevitable chance meetings at the hospital she had hardly seen him. Maggie drew attention to the fact one evening when they were having a coffee together after coming off duty.

'I've been meaning to ask you, what happened to your budding affair with the gorgeous Dr Bonham?' she asked. 'I thought things were getting off the ground there, but I haven't heard you mention any more dates with him.'

Claire shrugged, trying to look unconcerned. 'I've hardly had time for dates with anyone, have I?' she said evasively. 'What with moving house and everything. Now that I live at home again and Mum has this new job, I have to do my share of the housework, you know.'

Maggie pulled a comic face. 'Poor little Cinderella, you'll have me in tears in a minute! Tell you what, when we get those results we'll have a night on the town.' She grinned. 'If I can find you a couple of rats and a pumpkin, that is! How about it?'

Claire pursed her lips. 'Better not count our chickens. Suppose we don't pass?'

Maggie gave a defiant snort. 'Think positively! If we fail we'll need that night on the town even more! Leave it to me. I'll book a table somewhere special.' She frowned. 'But you still haven't answered my question. What went wrong between you and Super Simon?'

'Nothing went wrong,' said Claire. 'There was nothing *to* go wrong. After all, it was only a casual dinner together. I have good reason to believe that there's already a special lady in his life, anyway.'

Maggie looked up at her sharply. 'If you're talking about who I think you are, I'd say *you* had first claim!' she said indignantly. 'You're not going to let *her* snitch him, are you?'

'What do you mean?' Claire frowned.

'Why, Gillian Blair, of course!' When Claire looked puzzled Maggie went on: 'Honestly, Claire, you must go around with your eyes and ears bunged up! Everyone's been speculating about those two for weeks now. I suppose it was inevitable, with their working together and both being so attractive.' She stopped, looking at Claire thoughtfully. 'If you weren't talking about her, who *were* you talking about?'

'No one special – it was just an impression.' Claire looked at her watch. 'Heavens, I must run. I promised to get something for supper on the way home.' She rose from the table, grateful for the excuse to get away from the awkward twists the conversation was taking. 'See you tomorrow – 'bye!'

She was crossing the hospital grounds five minutes later when she saw them – Simon and Dr Gillian Blair, standing talking together near the car park entrance. Gillian was showing him something. It looked like a piece of paper. She looked slightly upset and Simon reached out to pat her shoulder, bending to smile into her face, as though he was trying to cheer her up. They were both too engrossed to notice Claire as she hurried past. All the way back to the flat she was deep in thought. So it looked as though Maggie had been right. There was a certain intimacy about the way their heads almost touched, in the tender concern in Simon's eyes as he looked at Gillian. The memory gave her a sharp pain. If only she hadn't been so stupid! She had had her chance and thrown it away, and now it was too late.

She stopped at the local supermarket to buy steak for their supper, impulsively adding a bottle of cheap wine to her trolley. She felt she needed something to cheer her up this evening. When she arrived at the flat with her loaded basket she found that the postman had been and there was a pile of mail behind the door. She dumped the basket on the hall table and sorted through it. Most of it seemed to be circulars and a few brown envelopes, no doubt containing bills. Then she saw it – the envelope addressed to her with the RCN insignia on the back. Her heart missed a beat as she stared down at it. A few square inches of paper, yet it held the answer to all those weeks of waiting – of years of hard work and studying. Taking a deep breath, she tore it open, but her eyes refused to focus on the typed words. They seemed to jump about on the paper.

'Darling, whatever is it? Here, give it to me.' Rosemary stepped through the door left open by Claire, and took the letter from her daughter's trembling hands. A moment later she looked up, her eyes shining. 'Oh! It's your results. You've *passed!*' She threw her arms round a stunned Claire. 'Oh, darling, I'm so proud of you! Staff Nurse Claire Simms – doesn't it sound grand?'

But somehow to Claire it all seemed unreal. Now that she had attained the goal she had been striving for the feeling of elation she had expected hadn't material- ised. Instead she felt numb and detached; as though the whole thing were happening to someone else. She stared dumbly at her mother. Why was it that all she could think of were those two heads close together, Simon's hand on Gillian Blair's shoulder and the expression in his eyes as he looked at her?

CHAPTER SEVEN

'Here's to us!' Maggie held her dry Martini high. 'The two best staff nurses Queen Eleanor's will ever have. And I don't care if this meal puts another stone on. It will have been worth it!'

Claire picked up her own glass and clinked it against Maggie's before taking a sip.

True to her word, Maggie had insisted on arranging the night out they had planned in celebration of passing their finals. Claire had left the choice of restaurant to her, somehow unable to summon up the necessary enthusiasm, but this evening when she had arrived to call for her Claire had been a little taken aback to discover that Maggie had booked a table at The Sailmaker's.

Sitting opposite in the intimate, candlelit room, she leaned back, looking around her with satisfaction. 'This is a great place, isn't it? I'd no idea it was so nice. Have you been here before?'

Claire played with the stem of her glass as

she said evasively: 'Oh, I came here once, some time ago.' She had nursed a vain hope that the evening would erase the memory of that date with Simon. But it wasn't working. The recollection of the evening they had sat at the table overlooking the river – and all that had happened later – was as painful as ever. She took a sip from her glass, then suddenly realised that Maggie was looking at her questioningly.

'What's up? You seem strangely quiet for a girl with something to celebrate. After all, things have been looking up for you lately, haven't they?'

'I'm fine. I suppose it's reaction,' she said, sipping her wine. 'Ever since I got my results I've felt sort of numb. Somehow I can't get as excited about it as I thought I would.'

Maggie nodded understandingly. 'I know what you mean. It's a bit of an anticlimax when it comes, isn't it?' She smiled up at the waiter as he put her food in front of her. 'Still, it's a jolly good excuse to forget the diet for a while, and that can't be bad, eh?' She picked up her knife and fork. 'Tell me, how is your mother enjoying her new job?'

Claire smiled. 'She loves it. Dr Phillips has been so helpful to her. It wasn't easy for her, getting used to a new job after all the years she worked in a solicitor's office, but he's helped a lot.'

Claire was glad that her moonlighting at Palmer's garage, along with the drama of the attempted robbery, had been successfully hushed up. Neither Maggie nor her mother knew of her involvement in it and, true to his word, Simon must have seen to it that she wasn't named in the newspapers, in spite of the ungrateful way she had lashed out at him. She had been so relieved, knowing perfectly well that the escapade would have earned her no sympathy at Queen Eleanor's. The sooner she could forget the whole incident, the better.

Maggie smiled, tucking into her food with relish. 'Great. Have you heard what ward they're sending you to?'

Claire shook her head. 'I should hear in the morning.' A movement at the other end of the room claimed her attention and she looked up to see a waiter coming towards them with two more customers following him. She froze with dismay when she saw who they were.

Dr Gillian Blair wore an elegantly cut black dress and the ash-blonde hair she usually wore in a smooth chignon flowed silkily about her shoulders. Behind her, Simon wore a dark suit. He looked so handsome that Claire felt her heart contract and she bit her lip, lowering her head as they drew closer. If she could have escaped she would gladly have done so, but there was nothing for it but to brazen the encounter out. It was clear that they were going to come face to face.

Gillian Blair saw them first and smiled. 'Hello – celebrating your success? Congratulations.'

Maggie thanked her while Claire raised her eyes slowly to Simon's. He met them steadily. 'I'd like to second that,' he said. 'I hope you have a pleasant evening.'

They passed on to their own table and Maggie let out a quiet exclamation: 'Phew, I'll bet that dress cost a bomb! And did you see those shoes? Everyone says she's got her hooks well and truly into him, but I must say they make a good-looking couple. She's very attractive and sexy, isn't she? Rumour has it that even her white coats have designer labels! I'd say she's a rival to be reckoned with. It's a good job you went off him.' She peered at Claire's flushed face. 'You *did* go off him, didn't you? You said you had.' She winced. 'Oh dear, I've put my big foot in it again, haven't I?'

Claire shook her head. 'Forget it. I'm

trying to.'

Maggie shrugged. 'Well, if you say so.' Her attention was on the table on the far side of the room where Simon and Dr Gillian had settled themselves. 'Hello, looks as though they're celebrating something too,' she said as a waiter brought a bottle of champagne in an ice-bucket to their table. 'He must have ordered that when he booked the table.' She narrowed her eyes speculatively. 'Now, what would *that* be about, do you suppose?'

Claire shrugged, trying to look unconcerned. 'I haven't the faintest idea, and I couldn't care less.'

'*Hey!* You don't think he might have popped the question, do you?' asked Maggie.

Claire's heart gave a painful twist, and Maggie looked up, catching the look in her eyes.

'Oh, sorry, love. That must have sounded like twisting the knife. You know, for all your protestations that you and he have nothing in common, I can still see how you feel about him.' She looked at her watch. 'Tell you what – let's go to the pictures. If we hurry we can still catch the last show. There's that new science fiction showing at the Plaza.'

Claire grinned bravely, permitting herself

a quick glance at the couple of the other side of the restaurant who seemed to be toasting each other. 'Good idea,' she said firmly. 'Let's get our bill.'

It was the following morning that she presented herself for duty on Wellington Ward, proudly wearing her new uniform complete with staff nurse's belt. She had been surprised to find herself assigned to the ophthalmic unit, but her nursing officer had told her that she had shown a marked aptitude for the work during her spell there during her training in Mr Fairbrother's clinic. Sister Baker seemed pleased to have her, and as the morning progressed she found herself enjoying her new status with all its responsibilities.

As the time for doctors' rounds drew near Claire found herself watching the glass doors at the end of the ward with more anticipation that she would have admitted to. At last she saw the familiar figure of Mr Fairbrother entering the ward, followed by Simon, and they began their round with Sister in attendance.

There were the usual number of routine cases – cataracts and glaucomas. One retinal detachment was awaiting surgery and at the end of the ward a new patient had been admitted the previous day, following examination at the eye clinic. It was as they reached her bed that Sister was called to the telephone and motioned to Claire to take over from her. As she joined the two doctors Mr Fairbrother turned to her with a smile.

'Congratulations, *Staff* Nurse Simms,' he said. 'I'm glad we're to have you here with us.' He glanced at Simon. 'It's by way of a double celebration. From now on we shall have to remember to address this gentleman as *Mr* Bonham.'

Claire smiled at Simon. 'Congratulations – sir.' Her heart gave a leap. So *that* was why he had been celebrating last night!

Mr Fairbrother smiled benignly at the patient. 'Now, Mrs Brampton, you couldn't have come into hospital at a better time. All these talented and ambitious young people waiting to do their best for you–' While he spoke he referred to his notes. 'I daresay Mr Bonham has explained your condition to you. It seems that at some time in the past you had a slight haemorrhage at the back of the eye. This caused scar tissue to form and over the years it has unfortunately pulled the retina away.'

The patient, a middle-aged woman, looked up at them anxiously. 'I didn't have any pain though, Doctor. It was just the flashes of light and the spots floating about. When I went to my optician I thought I might be needing new glasses. I never thought it was anything serious.'

Mr Fairbrother smiled. 'Try not to worry. You're in very good hands.' He looked at Simon. 'This is Mr Bonham, whom you met yesterday at the eye clinic. It was he who recommended you for immediate admission. I'm going to leave you in his able hands, as he has made a recent study of retinal detachment and will be performing your operation.'

As Mr Fairbrother moved on to the next bed the patient looked at Simon. 'Why did I have to come in right away, Doctor?' she asked. 'Is this condition dangerous? I'm not likely to lose my sight, am I?'

Simon perched himself on the edge of the bed. 'I don't want you to worry, Mrs Brampton, but we're going to run some tests on you over the next few days to try to ascertain the reason for your visual difficulties. You may be moved to another ward, but you needn't let that concern you. Now, I'd like to ask you some questions.'

Claire listened carefully to what he asked and drew her own conclusions. As they moved away she looked at him.

'You suspect diabetes?'

He nodded. 'Yes, though it's recent and therefore not the cause of the detachment. We took some blood and urine tests when she was admitted, and I'd like to know the results as soon as possible. If she's positive she'll have to be moved, of course. If not I'd like her to be on this week's list.'

'What are the chances of that being possible?' asked Claire.

He shook his head. 'Not good, I'm afraid.'

As they reached the end of the ward he looked round for Mr Fairbrother who was still chatting to one of his elderly patients at the far end. 'I'm glad you passed your finals, Claire,' he told her, lowering his voice. 'I hope your family problems have been happily sorted out now.'

'Thank you, they have.' Claire moistened her dry lips. 'I – never thanked you for what you did. I was lucky not to have had more publicity – of the unwelcome sort.'

He shrugged. 'It was nothing. I–' What he was about to say Claire never discovered for at that moment the door at the end of the ward opened and Dr Gillian Blair appeared, looking immaculate and pretty in her well cut white coat. Claire couldn't help noticing the way she looked at Simon as she joined them. Muttering an excuse, Claire moved away, acutely aware that her presence was no longer needed.

It was just after lunch that Sister called her into the office. 'I've just had the results of Mrs Brampton's tests back from the path lab,' she said, 'and they're positive. Mr Bonham has suggested that she attends the diabetic clinic this afternoon, and as she seems rather taken with you, perhaps it would be a good idea if you took her down. Before you go, you'd better have a little talk with her. She should be prepared for the fact that she may be diabetic, and I'm sure you know what to say.'

Claire didn't relish the 'little talk'. She didn't know the patient well. Perhaps she was the type who became upset easily – could she handle it tactfully? It wasn't easy to break the news to a patient that she almost certainly had a complaint that was likely to remain with her for the rest of her life.

Mrs Brampton was sitting in the day room alone. Claire went in and closed the door. 'It will soon be time to go down for your tests, Mrs Brampton,' she said. 'I thought I'd just come and prepare you for what's likely to happen.'

The woman looked up at her calmly. 'The doctor thinks I'm diabetic, doesn't he?'

Claire was stunned. 'Well, that is what the tests are for. A safety precaution. But how did you know?'

'A close friend of mine had it, and I guessed from the questions the doctor asked this morning.'

'Did you ever go to the diabetic clinic with her?' asked Claire. The woman shook her head.

'No, and I must admit that I'm not looking forward to it. Will you come with me?'

'Sister has already suggested that I do,' Claire told her with a smile.

At the diabetic clinic Mrs Brampton was weighed, after which more blood and urine samples were taken. Finally she was examined by Dr Phillips, who took her blood pressure, listened to her heart, took a further blood sample to test for kidney function and finally examined her eyes again with the aid of an ophthalmoscope.

'As you already know, you have a detached retina, Mrs Brampton,' he told her, 'but it has nothing to do with your diabetes, which is relatively recent. Can you remember whether you've ever had a severe blow to the head?'

The patient considered for a long moment before she said: 'I was involved in a car accident some years ago. I had concussion at the time, but it wasn't serious – or so I thought.'

Dr Phillips nodded. 'That could do it. It wasn't the injury, you see, but the scar tissue that caused the trouble.' He smiled cheerfully. 'However, we have a wonderful ophthalmic team here at Queen Eleanor's and once we get your diabetes under control you'll be able to have it put right in no time. For the time being I think you can go home once we have you stabilised. You'll be getting a visit, from our Diabetic Health Visitor, who will explain everything to you – help you to get used to injecting yourself with the insulin and so on.'

On the way back to the ward Mrs Brampton was apprehensive. 'I'm sure I'll never be able to give myself injections,' she said.

Claire gave her arm a reassuring squeeze. 'Oh yes, you will. All the diabetics I know manage beautifully. The DHV will tell you if there's a local diabetic group you can join, and there's the British Diabetic Association too. You don't have to struggle with it alone, you know.'

Claire was crossing the car park on her way home that evening when a car drew up beside her and she turned to see Simon's silver-grey saloon. He wound down the window.

'Hello. Get in, I'll take you home.'

She shook her head. 'It's all right. It's such a beautiful evening, I'd rather walk. We live close enough now, you know.'

'I do know.' Without another word he swung the car into an empty parking space and got out, while she stood watching him uncertainly.

He shook his head, giving her a wry smile. 'So – if the mountain won't come to Mohammed–' He fell into step beside her. 'Shall we go round by the road, or take the short cut through the woods?'

She shrugged. 'I don't mind, but I don't really see–'

'I want to talk to you,' he said abruptly. 'It's important.' He took her arm.

The woods that surrounded the hospital were mostly of pine and other evergreens. Here and there rhododendrons clustered, just coming into glorious bloom. High among the branches of the tallest trees the blackbirds were throwing their full-throated evening song at the sky. Claire tried hard to keep her heart from joining them as she walked, acutely aware of Simon's hand, warm about her arm.

He stopped as they came to a rough bench under the trees. 'Let's sit here for a moment.'

She hesitated. 'I really should be getting back. It's my turn to start the meal–' She broke off as he sat down, pulling her down beside him.

'I told you, I want to talk to you.' He looked at her thoughtfully. 'Maybe you've heard rumours about a new ophthalmic unit?'

Claire shook her head, frowning. 'I thought the project had been shelved.'

He nodded. 'It seems that plans have been put forward for enlarging the existing unit. We need the extra beds and this way would save a considerable amount of money. The plans have been passed and the work will be started very soon.'

Claire smiled. 'That's good.' She was still wondering why he was telling her this when he suddenly laid a hand on her arm, bending forward to look into her eyes.

'You haven't understood, Claire. It means that the unit will have to close until the work is finished, which will probably be about three months. All ophthalmic cases will be sent over to St Winifred's in Coleford. I understand there'll be vacancies for a limited number of nurses there, but they'll be expected to travel as there's no accommodation available.'

Claire's heart sank. Now she saw the point. Coleford was twenty miles away – and her mother had just sold her car! Just when their problems seemed to have sorted themselves out here was another. She drew a deep sigh.

'Oh dear, Fate seems to have it in for me.' She turned to look at him. 'Thank you for telling me.' Her heart was heavy. When Simon had suggested a walk she might have known it wasn't the pleasure of her company he wanted.

'There is another alternative, though I don't know quite how you'll feel about it,' he said hesitantly.

She looked at him. 'What is it?'

'A sabbatical,' he told her. 'How would you feel about taking a short-term private case?'

She stared at him in surprise. 'It's something I've never thought about. Anyway, I don't know how the powers that be would view it.'

'You can leave that side of it to me,' he told her abruptly. 'If you want the job I think I can safely say it's yours. It's ophthalmic, of course, and the patient is diabetic. That's why I thought you would be ideal – I know you're interested in diabetes.'

'I am. Is the patient female?' asked Claire. He nodded.

'If you like I'll take you to see her. I have a feeling you'll get along together.'

Claire was silent. There were a dozen questions she wanted to ask, but she settled for just one: 'How can you be so sure that I'd be allowed back here afterwards?' she asked.

'You will. Trust me.'

She bit her lip. 'Is it far from here?'

Simon smiled. 'You're thinking of your mother, aren't you?' He looked at her wryly. 'At the risk of seeming interfering, I think it's time you thought about what's best for you. She has a job now – and a new flat. I take it there are no more problems with your young brother?' Claire shook her head, and he smiled. 'You have nothing to worry about then. The patient – Miss Lattimer – lives on the coast, only about twelve miles from here. I'm sure you could have the use of a car so that you could drive over and visit.'

'I'd – like time to think about it,' she said slowly.

'Of course. Talk it over with your mother and see how you feel.' He took a slip of paper out of his pocket. 'Here is the patient's name and address. You can contact her direct if you like. Or if you want any more details you can ring me.'

Over the next few days Claire gave a lot of thought to Simon's proposition, talking it over with her mother and her nursing officer. Finally they all agreed that it might be the best course in the circumstances. Claire rang Simon's number several times but could get no reply. He was having a few days off, so she didn't see him at the hospital. Eventually she decided to go round to his flat to ask him some questions regarding the job.

It was early evening when she climbed the stairs of the Georgian house she had visited only once before. Her heart quickened as she rang the bell and stood waiting for Simon to open the door. Would he think it a cheek of her to call round like this? She rehearsed her explanations silently as she waited. As the door began to open she moistened her lips and took a deep breath, ready to begin, but she was brought up smartly by the unexpected sight that faced her. Looking up, she found herself looking into the eyes of Gillian Blair. Her hair hung loose about her shoulders and her legs and feet were bare. She wore a silky négligé, the belt of which she was still hastily tying.

'Oh, hello. Can I help you?' she asked.

Claire stared speechlessly at her for a moment, then shook her head, muttering an unintelligible reply. Turning, she made a panic-stricken dash for the stairs, in an agony of embarrassment and humiliation.

CHAPTER EIGHT

Claire looked around her as she stepped off the bus. She was standing on the village green, in the centre of which was a painted sign bearing the village's name: Fritcham-on-Sea. Cottages, small shops and a thatched pub called The Cricketers looked on to the green which was bordered by chestnut trees, now in glorious pink and white bloom.

She had telephoned Phyllis Lattimer a few days ago and between them they had arranged today's meeting. Claire took the piece of paper Simon had given her out of her handbag and looked at the address: Pilgrim's House. There was no street name, so obviously she would have to ask someone. She called out to a boy cycling past:

'Can you tell me where Pilgrim's House is, please?'

He stopped and got off his bicycle. 'It's a good way from here, near the sea. You take the beach road.' He pointed. 'Over there, past the church and first right.' He looked down at her shoes in the pitying way that country people reserve for townees. 'Part of it's pretty rough walking.'

'Oh dear. I suppose there isn't a bus?' asked Claire without much hope.

The boy shook his head. 'Only one bus a day here, miss, and that don't go anywhere near the beach – just into town and back.'

'How far is it?'

He scratched his head. 'I dunno. Must be a mile and a half – maybe two.'

Not for the first time, Claire mourned the going of her mother's Mini. She thanked the boy and set off. But the walk wasn't as bad as she had feared. There was so much to see – pretty cottages, fields and hedges, alive with wild life and, presently, the first heart-lifting glimpse of the sea, a sparkling blue ribbon crowning the horizon. The boy had been right about the last part of the walk, though. The road, never more than a narrow lane, finally petered out into a rutted sandy track. The heels of Claire's smart shoes sank into it, making walking difficult, and she was relieved when at last a house came into view.

It stood facing grassy dunes on the far side of which Claire could see a strip of sandy beach washed by frothing waves. Now a salty breeze greeted her, lifting her hair and tugging at the skirt of her coat. The name of the house was on the white-painted gate, and she pushed it open gratefully and began to walk up the shingled drive.

The house had quite clearly been added to by various owners down the years. The original middle section was built of stone, now weathered by the sea winds. Perhaps a century later a wing had been added on either side of this, built this time of the brick and split flint so beloved of Norfolk builders; later still a new front entrance had been built, this time of mellowed brick with a stout oak door, and it was on this that Claire knocked.

The woman who answered invited her in and showed her into a sunny drawing room at the back of the house. Claire's first impression was of soft pastel shades – twin settees flanking an Adam fireplace and a grand piano standing in a deep recess opposite.

'Miss Lattimer will be with you in a minute,' the woman told her in a soft Norfolk burr. 'Perhaps you'd like a cup of tea after your long walk?'

Claire said she would. Wandering round the room, she looked at the photographs set out on a little antique writing desk; they were mostly of a little boy in various stages of his childhood. Walking over to the French windows, she looked out on to a pretty garden, still bright with late spring flowers. She tried to imagine herself living and working here.

She hadn't been waiting for more than a few minutes when the door opened and Phyllis Lattimer came in. She was a tall, slim woman in, Claire guessed, her late fifties. Her silver hair was elegantly coiffured and it wasn't hard to imagine that she had once been very beautiful. She held out her hand to Claire, smiling a charming welcome.

'I was so pleased to get your telephone call. How good of you to come all this way to see me,' she said. 'On the bus too! The walk from the Green must have quite exhausted you.' She indicated one of the settees. 'Please, sit down and rest.'

Claire seated herself. 'Thank you. I'm not really tired though, there was so much to see. This is a very lovely place to live.'

'Perhaps you wouldn't like it quite so much in the winter!'

The door opened and the woman who had shown Claire in came in with a tray of tea which she set down on a table drawn up

155

before the fireplace.

'This is Mrs Winters who comes in to help me each day,' said Phyllis Lattimer. 'I really don't know what I'd do without her.' The woman withdrew and she smiled, starting to pour the tea. 'Do have one of Mrs Winters' delicious little cakes, Miss Simms.'

'Please call me Claire. Miss Simms sounds so formal.' Claire took the cup handed to her.

The older woman smiled. 'I agree about formality. You must call me Phyllis. Now, down to business. As you'll have gathered, I live here alone. I used to share with a friend, but she has just remarried. I don't know anyone else I feel I could share my home with, but since I've contracted this tiresome eye trouble I need to have someone around – for a while at least. I'm diabetic and I have this wretched retinopathy thing, for which I hope to have surgery soon.'

Claire nodded. 'I understand'

'You said you were taking a sabbatical from Queen Eleanor's?'

'Yes. I have a letter from my nursing officer,' Claire told her. 'And one from Mr Fairbrother who is the ophthalmologist there. I do have some experience in diabetic problems.'

Phyllis smiled. 'And I daresay that by the time you've seen me through my op you'll have a lot more!'

Claire glanced towards the piano. 'Do you play?'

The other woman smiled ruefully. 'Oh dear, you make me feel old! There was a time when the name Phyllis Lattimer was known to everyone.'

Claire blushed, feeling that she had made a gaffe, but Phyllis Lattimer shook her head. 'I didn't mean to embarrass you, my dear. It's a long time since I gave my last concert. I only play now to amuse myself.'

Wanting to change the subject, Claire looked at the photographs on the writing desk. 'Is the little boy a relative?' she asked.

Phyllis smiled. 'My son. He's grown up now and refuses to have his photograph taken, so I cherish those. He was such a sweet little boy.' She shook her head. 'I regret how much I missed of his childhood. I was travelling so extensively in those days, with my music. He was brought up by other people and then away at school. I don't think he's ever quite forgiven me for not making a secure home for him.' She took a sip of her tea, looking at Claire over the rim of her cup. 'My marriage broke up while he was still a baby, you see. It didn't stand the pressure of my career, I'm afraid. That was when I reverted to my single name, though of course I'd always used it professionally.'

'Oh dear, I'm sorry,' muttered Claire, burying her face in her cup. So far she seemed to be bringing up all the wrong subjects!

'I've been hoping he'd marry and give me some grandchildren I could spoil,' Phyllis went on, 'but he doesn't seem in any hurry to do so. There was a girl once, a long time ago, a lovely girl. I had great hopes then and I believe he was very much in love with her, but she left him in favour of an older man with more money.' She sighed. 'Sometimes I feel that the women in his life have given him a rather a poor view of the opposite sex.' She smiled. 'But enough of that. Tell me something about yourself.'

Claire briefly sketched her own background for her prospective employer, giving priority to her nursing experience. When she had finished Phyllis Lattimer nodded.

'I think we're going to get along admirably together, my dear. If you agree I'd like you to begin as soon as possible.' She rose from the settee opposite Claire. 'Come and see your room – I think you'll like it. Then I'll get Mrs Winters to drive you back to the village.' She glanced at her watch. 'You'll be just in time to catch the bus as it comes back from town.'

As Claire followed her up the staircase she added: 'If you decide to come and look after me you'll have full use of the car whenever you want it.' She turned with a sad smile. 'I'm not allowed to drive at the moment, you see.'

On the journey back to Kingsmere Claire had a lot of thinking to do. She had already decided to take the job. She liked Phyllis Lattimer very much and felt sure they would get along together. There was no problem about her job at Queen's Eleanor's; her nursing officer had assured her that it would be waiting for her once the new ophthalmic unit was opened. Nursing Phyllis Lattimer would only serve to widen her experience. But there was another reason for wanting to get away from Kingsmere. It was crystal clear now that Simon's relationship with Dr Gillian Blair was serious, Sally or no Sally! Being forced to stand by and watch it develop would be much too painful to bear. Maybe a three-month respite at Fritcham, right away from Simon and everything connected with him, would help her to get over him.

It was a few days later, during Mr Fair-brother's round, when Simon sought her out. She had made herself scarce, making an excuse to go to Sister's office for some notes. She had just collected them from the filing cabinet when he came into the office and closed the door. Claire spun round, feeling trapped.

'Oh!– These notes – Mr Fairbrother may be needing them,' she muttered.

He shook his head. 'He isn't, and you know it.' There was a determined look about his mouth as he stepped closer to her. 'I want to know what's the matter,' he demanded.

Claire swallowed, her mouth suddenly dry. 'The matter?' she echoed. 'Nothing, as far as I know.'

His brows came together in a frown. 'Then why are you avoiding me?'

'I'm not – that's absurd.' She made to walk past him, but he grasped her wrist.

'I understand you've taken the job I recommended.'

She nodded, a little taken aback at his knowing.

'I would have taken you over to meet your new patient if you'd asked,' he told her. 'I did say I'd help.'

She looked at him directly, trying hard not to sound accusing as she said: 'I tried to get in touch, but you weren't – available. I rang, and then – and then I went round to your flat.' She wrenched her wrist from his grasp. 'I shouldn't have done that – I'm sorry. I had no idea, you see – about – about–' She found herself quite unable to finish the sentence and it petered out as she fumbled with the sheaf of notes in her hand. Simon stared at her for a moment, his brows drawn together. He had just opened his mouth to say something when the door opened and Sister Baker looked in.

'Mr Fairbrother would like to discuss something with you, Mr Bonham.' She held the door open for Simon to pass through, raising an eyebrow at Claire behind his back. The moment was over, leaving Claire feeling limp.

When she went for her lunch break she found Steve Lang waiting for her in the canteen.

'What's all this I hear about you leaving Queen E's?' he asked, settling himself opposite her.

She shook her head. 'Not leaving – only taking a sabbatical while the new ophthalmic unit is being built.'

He cocked an eyebrow at her. 'And what am I going to do without my favourite fiancée, may I ask?'

Claire shrugged. 'Maybe it's time you got yourself another – for real this time.'

'Ah, but there'll never be another like you,' said Steve, leaning forward and gazing into her eyes.

She shot him an impatient look. 'Not now, Steve,' she warned, 'all that wears a bit thin after a while, you know.'

He reached for her hand across the table. 'It might give you a big laugh to know that it's more than half true,' he told her. 'A lot more!'

She looked up and saw that his face was serious. 'I really do think a lot of you, Claire,' he said quietly. 'I didn't realise just how much till I heard you were going. I've led you a bit of a dance one way and another, but I think you know that it was just my fun.'

She extricated her hand and began to eat her lunch. 'Of course I know, Steve. But I'm sure you'll find someone else to tease.'

'Oh, come on now. You know it's more than that. I–'

'Do you mind if I join you?'

Claire looked up in surprise to see Simon standing by their table.

'Aren't there any other tables?' Steve asked pointedly.

Simon ignored him, drawing out a chair and sitting down, his eyes fixed on Claire. For a moment there was silence, then Steve shrugged resignedly.

'I'll ring you this evening,' he said sulkily, and got up to leave.

When he had gone Simon looked at Claire. 'I'm sorry about that, but it was the only way. I only have a minute. Are you free this evening?' he was looking at her intently. 'Will you have dinner with me? I'd like to talk to you.'

She shook her head. 'I don't know what there can be to talk about. Besides, what about – about Dr Blair?'

He looked surprised. 'Dr Blair? What does she have to do with it?'

She stared at him. 'You should know that better than I.'

He shook his head, then looked at his watch. 'Look, there's no time to talk now. I'll pick you up at eight.' He stood up. 'I'll see you later,' he told her firmly.

Claire watched him go, hating herself for not putting up more of a fight. He seemed to take it for granted that she was free – just waiting for him to ask her out. Yet maybe it was as well for them to talk. She would be able to tell him what she thought of a man who collected women as though they were butterflies. First Sally, then Gillian – if he thought he could get her to join his collection he had another think coming, and she would make sure he knew it!

It was a fine evening, and when she came off duty Claire decided to walk back to the flat she shared with her mother. She had just set off when there was a call behind her and, turning, she saw Maggie running to catch her up.

'Hi!' she panted with the exertion as she caught up to Claire. 'Where are you off to in such a hurry? Don't tell me – you've got a date.'

Claire smiled. 'I have, as a matter of fact. There's no hurry, though.'

Maggie fell into step beside her. 'In that case come up to my room for a coffee. We haven't had a really good natter for ages and I want to hear all about this new job of yours.'

Claire smiled. 'All right, though there isn't that much to tell.'

'Not what I heard,' Maggie told her. 'A car of your own – luxury flat, use of the swimming pool–'

Claire laughed. 'Oh, that grapevine! I'm to have the *use* of a car, a nice *room* of my own, and as for the swimming pool–'

Maggie threw up her hands in mock horror. 'Oh no! Don't tell me there isn't one. I couldn't stand the disillusionment!'

'Only the biggest in the world,' teased Claire. 'The only snag is I have to share it with the Merchant Navy, the Royal Navy and a few million fishes! It's the North Sea!'

Maggie laughed and tucked her arm through Claire's. 'I do miss having you next door at the Nurses' Home,' she confided. 'I'm sure you must miss hearing all the gossip.'

Claire shook her head. 'Not really. I miss your company, though.'

Once inside her room Maggie closed the door and put the kettle on. 'You'll have heard the latest about the lovely Dr Gillian, I suppose?'

Claire nodded. So it was all over the hospital! 'I found out by accident.'

Maggie set out the cups and saucers, her back to Claire. 'I have to admit I was surprised, weren't you?'

Claire shrugged. Simon's affair with Dr Gillian Blair was the last thing she wanted to discuss. With a sudden flash of inspiration she introduced the one sure-fire subject-changer she knew:

'You know you really have lost weight, Maggie. What diet are you on at the moment?'

It did the trick, and the rest of the time was spent discussing the merits of a calorie-controlled diet versus low carbohydrate intake.

Rosemary Simms was working late, catching up on the backlog of work that had accumulated while David Phillips had been without a secretary, so Claire had the flat to herself. She showered and washed her hair, then stood in front of the open wardrobe, trying to make up her mind what to wear. At last she decided on the dress she had just bought to wear to Mike's Speech Day next week. It was made of a silky material in a subtle shade of rose pink. Its skirt swirled prettily about her hips, its colour lending her pale complexion a soft, translucent glow. Looking out of the window, she saw Simon's car draw up outside just on eight o'clock and, letting herself out of the flat, she ran down to meet him.

She had wondered if he would take her to The Sailmaker's again, but as he headed the car on to the bypass in the direction of the coast, she soon realised that wasn't their destination. As he drove Simon was silent and she glanced at his profile, trying to assess his mood. It wasn't possible. He seemed to be intent upon the road. She took in the smooth line of his jaw, the firm, slightly square chin and well-moulded mouth. With a sudden quickening of her pulse she was reminded of its warmth on hers and tore her eyes away, biting her lip. She forced her mind on to more mundane subjects, wondering what Dr Gillian was doing this evening. Cleaning the flat, maybe – or washing out Simon's socks!

'What a strange expression you're wearing! You must be having some very dark thoughts. Want to share them?'

Claire blushed as she realised that Simon had been glancing at her for the past few minutes. She shrugged. 'They're not worth sharing,' she said dismissively, looking out of the window. 'Where are we going?'

'A little place I've recently discovered,' he told her. 'I think you'll like it. We're almost there.'

The 'little place' turned out to be the

Poacher's Inn, a restaurant converted from an ancient stone barn. It stood in the grounds of a farmhouse and they drove to it along a winding road. Simon parked the car and came round to open the door for her. As she got out she stumbled a little on the loose stones and his hand closed around her arm. She looked up, unable to avoid his eyes any longer.

'It's been a long time since we last dined together, Claire,' he said. 'I still haven't worked out just what went wrong, you know.'

His eyes held hers almost hypnotically and just for a moment she forgot all the barriers between them. 'Perhaps – perhaps we'd better go in – if you've booked a table, that is,' she muttered. For a moment he hesitated, then he nodded in agreement.

'You're right. Let's eat, we can talk later.'

All through the meal Claire was acutely aware that their communication was on two levels. On the surface their talk was light and pleasant, but they were both conscious of the unasked questions that would come later. Claire wondered what turn the conversation would take. Did Simon imagine that she didn't know about his relationship with Gillian Blair? How could he be so naive as to

168

think one could keep a thing like that quiet in an environment like Queen Eleanor's?

When they came out of the restaurant it was dark. As he joined her in the car she thanked him politely for a pleasant evening, and he turned in his seat, looking at her as though she had just insulted him.

'How formal and polite! Not at all the way you sound when you're with Steve Lang. What is it, Claire? Why are you so inhibited with me?' His arm, which lay along the back of the seat, dropped on to her shoulders and she felt it tighten as he drew her closer. 'The last time we were alone together–'

Her heart was beating fast. His face was almost touching hers, she could feel the warmth of his breath on her cheek. In a moment he would kiss her and her resolve would melt helplessly. She wouldn't be able to say any of the things she meant to. She couldn't – mustn't let it happen. 'Where's Dr Blair this evening?' she asked suddenly as his lips came closer. To her own ears her voice sounded unnaturally high, almost shrill. He frowned, raising his head to look down at her.

'She's on duty,' he said. 'Why are you so interested in Dr Blair?'

She shrugged. 'I'm not. I – just wondered.'

169

Without another word Simon withdrew his arm and started the engine, turning the car to drive back down the long winding drive and on to the road. After a few moments he glanced at her.

'You'll come back to my place for coffee?'

Claire moistened her dry lips. 'Oh! – I don't know.'

He pressed his foot down positively on the accelerator and the car sprang forward. 'I shall take it that means yes.'

She stole a glance at his profile. The light was dim, but she could see that he was angry. But *why?* Surely if anyone was angry it should be Gillian Blair; especially if she came back to the flat and found Claire there? She shuddered, hot with embarrassment at the very thought.

They reached the outskirts of Kingsmere and Simon began to negotiate the complicated traffic system. It was several minutes after they had passed the hospital that Claire turned to look at him.

'Where are we going?' she asked, puzzled. 'You said your place.'

He behaved as though he hadn't heard her and she looked out of the window at the unfamiliar streets. They were in a part of the town she didn't know, a fairly new small estate of trim houses. They pulled up at the end of a cul-de-sac and Simon got out, coming round to open her door. She looked up at him.

'Who lives here?'

Still without answering he took her arm and led her firmly up to the front door, producing a key and opening it. Then he turned to her. 'Well, are you coming in?'

As she stepped into the hall he switched on the light and opened another door, leading to a smartly furnished lounge. Suddenly he laughed.

'I wish you could see your face!' He grasped her by the shoulders. 'I can't think why it took so long for the penny to drop with me! You thought I'd asked Gillian to move in with me, didn't you – thought we were having an affair?'

She shook her head, colouring hotly. 'I – well, I–'

'Of course you did! I should have realised when you said you'd been to see me. Is that what all this has been about?'

'You – mean this house is yours?' she whispered.

'Yes. It's small, private and convenient. A real home – just what I've always wanted, and Gillian needed a flat so she jumped at the chance of getting my old one.' He gave her a wry grin. 'Shall I make a confession to you? The previous owners of this bought your old house in Sycamore Avenue.'

Claire's mouth dropped open as she looked up into his eyes. 'So it was *you* who engineered the whole thing! No wonder it all happened quickly!' A thought struck her and she narrowed her eyes at him. 'Were you responsible for Mum getting the job with Dr Phillips too?'

He held up his hands. 'Not guilty. At least, only in part – for drawing her attention to it.'

Claire stared at him. 'You and she have been doing all this behind my back!'

'You *did* tell me to stop interfering in your life,' he reminded her.

She bit her lip. 'Don't remind me. But why, Simon?' she asked softly. 'Why did you do all that for me?'

For a long moment he looked down at her. 'Do I really have to tell you that?' he asked. His arms reached out for her, drawing her close. His lips were warm and firm as they claimed hers, drawing from her a response that grew till it made her senses reel. When at last his mouth left hers he drew a sigh.

'I wanted so much to help you, but you

were so fiercely independent,' he said, his lips against her hair. 'I admired your loyalty to your family and your spirit with one half of me while the other half wanted to shake you! That night when I saw you working at the garage I was taking Gillian to look at the flat. I came back to talk to you.' His arms tightened round her. 'I can't describe how I felt when I saw what was about to happen. Something just seemed to take me over, and I didn't stop – to think – I just ploughed in.'

'You probably saved my life,' whispered Claire. 'And then all I could do was tell you to stop interfering.'

He kissed her forehead. 'Forget it,' he told her. 'The sooner the better.'

'Everyone is saying what a handsome couple you and Dr Gillian make,' she whispered.

He laughed. 'I might have known the gossips would get busy! What they didn't discover was that Gillian had a fiancé up in Scotland. He's a GP and he's planning to move south as soon as he can so that they can be married.'

She looked up at him. 'You took her out to celebrate your Fellowship,' she said, thinking of the pain that evening had caused her. 'You had champagne!'

He laughed softly. 'Oh, Claire! It was her birthday. The champagne was from her fiancé. She asked *me* out to dinner because she had no one to celebrate with – not the other way around. Most of the evening I had to sit and listen to the merits of the wonderful Dr Tim Gardner! I kept stealing a look at you across the room, but you looked so cool. You didn't seem to care.'

She stared at him incredulously. If he only knew! Reaching up, she wound her arms around his neck. 'I cared,' she said simply.

They made coffee and carried the tray into the trim lounge, where Claire made herself comfortable on a cushion at Simon's feet, her head on his knee as he settled himself on the settee.

'One thing puzzles me. I don't quite understand how you knew about Sally,' he said.

Claire blushed. 'There was a phone call – that night at your flat, while you were trying to borrow some milk from your neighbour. I was looking for a pencil and I found the photograph in a drawer. I took it that she was the caller too.'

He shook his head. 'Couldn't have been. Sally lives in America. I haven't set eyes on her for years.' He reached out to stroke her hair. 'I met her when I was still a student. She worked as a secretary at the hospital where her father was a consultant. She finally married one of his patients, a wealthy American business man.'

'You kept her photograph,' said Claire, remembering the florid inscription. He smiled.

'Why not? We were friends for a long time. I used to hear from her quite regularly.'

'Were you very much in love with her?' Claire asked in a small voice. 'Are you still – a little?'

Suddenly Simon bent forward to cup her chin. His fingers were hard against her jawbone and the eyes that searched hers were dark.

'Do you never take anything or anyone on trust, Claire?' he asked. Wide-eyed, she looked up at him without answering and he bent and kissed her hard. Arms around her, he drew her up on to the settee, cradling her in his arms. His kisses were searching and possessive, but his hands were gentle and sensuous as they caressed her, stirring her senses to heights she had never before experienced. If she had nursed any doubts he quickly dispelled them, making her forget everything but the fierce longing that took possession of her. The coffee remained unpoured on the coffee table as the world faded into insignificance around them.

CHAPTER NINE

St Crispin's Speech Day was a day Rosemary Simms had never missed since her son had been a pupil at the school, but this year she was forced to make an exception, as she explained to Claire over breakfast the following Sunday morning.

'David has been so good, putting up with my mistakes while I've been easing into the job,' she said, staring into her coffee cup, her forehead furrowed with anxiety. 'There was a time when I thought I would have to give it up, but he's been so patient. Now that I've cleared the backlog and I'm getting into my stride, I'm really beginning to enjoy working for him.'

Claire looked at her mother. She hadn't missed the use of the consultant's name – 'David' – but she made no mention of it. 'I'm sure he wouldn't mind you having a day off,' she said, but Rosemary shook her head.

'I didn't tell you – that's the day he's speaking at the BDA conference in London.

He wants me to go with him.'

'I see. Well, I'm sure Mike will understand,' Claire assured her. 'I can go, so at least one of us will be there, and he isn't a baby any longer, after all.'

But her mother still looked doubtful. 'I can't help worrying. He didn't seem at all himself during the Easter holidays, and when he rang last night he sounded – I don't know – decidedly strange. Not like Mike at all.'

'He's growing up, Mum,' Claire pointed out gently. 'He's getting to the age when he doesn't confide so much – beginning to cope with his own problems.'

'Problems?' Rosemary looked up in alarm. 'Has he said something to you? What do you mean, problems?'

Claire laughed, though she felt a small stab of impatience with her mother. 'There you go again!' she told her. 'You're too tense. Growing boys hate that. Mike's a teenager now and a more than usually clever one. You'll have to face the fact that he doesn't need us as much as he once did.' She reached across the table to touch her mother's hand. 'It's a *good* sign, Mum. Surely you realise that?'

Rosemary shook her head, trying to laugh.

'I suppose so. It doesn't make it any easier, though – knowing he's growing up, coming to terms with the fact that one day in the not so distant future I'll be facing life alone.'

Claire pressed the fingers that she held. It wasn't like her mother to be depressed, though she knew, of course, that there were times when she missed her husband's love and support desperately. 'Surely you don't think that either Mike or I would let that happen?' she said quietly.

Her mother looked up, a shamefaced expression in her eyes. 'Oh, don't take any notice of me,' she said, getting up and beginning to clear the table. 'It's just that sometimes it's difficult to know what to do for the best. Like when Mr Bonham offered his help with the house sale and told me about the job with David – Dr Phillips. He warned me that you'd be cross if you knew. I felt so guilty, keeping it from you, yet what was I to do? It felt so *good*, having a man advising me again. Sometimes being independent can be a struggle.'

Claire sighed as she rose to help with the washing-up. 'It was very good of him. I was the stupid one. All that's sorted out now, Mum, so don't worry.'

Her mother turned to look at her. 'I –

rather gathered that he thinks highly of you. You say it's all sorted out. Does that mean–?'

'It means we're now good friends,' said Claire firmly. 'Though I doubt if I'll be seeing very much of him for the next three months – while I'm at Fritcham. We'll be working so far apart.'

Rosemary dried her hands. Looking thoughtfully at her daughter, she asked: 'You don't regret taking the job?'

Claire shrugged noncommittally. 'Again, it was Simon's idea.' Her eyebrows rose as something suddenly occurred to her. 'He seems to be running our lives at the moment, doesn't he?'

She made the journey to St Crispin's by train and arrived in time to take Mike out to lunch at The Haycock, the local village pub close to the school, a treat he usually enjoyed. The Speech Day ceremony and prize giving was to take place in the afternoon. He had greeted her enthusiastically enough, but she noticed that he attacked the meal with less than his usual zest and that he seemed preoccupied. At last she asked:

'Are you all right, Mike? You usually eat enough for the whole school. Not disappointed about Mum not being able to come, are you?'

He shook his head, looking up at her unhappily. 'As a matter of fact I'm glad she isn't here. This is the first year I haven't taken a prize.'

She laughed. 'Is *that* what's worrying you? As if we care whether you get one or not! You can't always be getting prizes, can you? I don't remember getting any at all when I was at school.'

But Mike looked no happier. 'Will you tell me the truth, Claire? Did Mum sell the house because of me – because of the fees going up?'

She tried to laugh it off. 'Of course not, silly–'

He interrupted to go on quickly: 'Because if she did it was an awful mistake. You see, I think it's a waste of money. I want to leave St Crispin's!'

Claire stared at her brother in amazement. 'Leave? But you've always loved it so much here!'

He pushed his barely touched plate away miserably. 'It wasn't so bad at first, though I was homesick, of course, but somehow it hasn't been the same since Dad died. Do you realise that in three years' time I could be earning myself?'

'Don't be so stupid, Mike,' Claire told him. 'You have a higher than average academic talent. You have a great future in front of you. It would be criminal to throw all that way. There's no need for you to worry about your school fees. Just work hard and make it worthwhile – Mum and I will take care of the worrying.'

'But that's just *it!* I'm nothing like as good as you think, Claire! I'll let you down and it'll all be for nothing in the end. I *have* to leave here! Don't you see, I can't stand the responsibility!'

The other diners in the small restaurant looked round curiously at the boy's outburst and he coloured miserably, sinking lower in his chair. 'I mean it,' he told Claire quietly.

She didn't know what to do about it. All through the ceremony that afternoon she sat, hardly hearing the speeches from now famous 'old boys'. There was an MP, an industrialist and a Cambridge don. She heard the laughter and the frequent bursts of applause, but her mind was with her younger brother and their conversation over lunch. At last she knew that before she left this afternoon she must see the Headmaster and ask his advice. That was what her mother would do if she were here. Claire thanked God that she wasn't; she was worried enough as it was.

Mr Cornish was desperately busy, but his secretary managed to get her a short interview with him for after tea. She made her excuses to Mike, pretending that she had to catch an early train, and sat waiting nervously outside the Head's study, listening to the clatter of his secretary's typewriter and hoping against hope that she would not have disquieting news to carry home to her mother.

At last the door opened and Mr Cornish cordially ushered a couple, obviously parents, out. He was a tall, spare man with a slight stoop and thinning grey hair. He looked at Claire and smiled.

'Ah, Miss Simms, do come in. I'm sorry to have kept you waiting. Speech Day, you know – always hectic.' He indicated a chair and closed the door, then sat down himself on the other side of his desk, looking up at her over the tops of his gold-rimmed half-spectacles.

'Well now, it's good to see you here – it means a lot to the boys to have their families here on Speech Day, you know. I was sorry your mother was unable to come.' He smiled. 'What can I do for you?'

Claire came straight to the point. 'Mike doesn't seem as happy here as he was. He seems despondent about his work. I'm afraid he's talking of leaving–' She stopped speaking as the smile left Mr Cornish's face. He took off his spectacles and polished them thoughtfully.

'Oh dear, I've been afraid of this.' He hooked the spectacles over his ears again and looked at Claire. 'He's quite right, I'm afraid. His work has fallen off this year. None of his masters can quite fathom why. Personally, I think it's delayed reaction to the death of his father, but he's a very sensitive boy, as I'm sure you know. Since the fees regrettably had to be increased he's been concerned about the distress it might cause at home. At least, that was the impression I received when I spoke to him.'

Claire was surprised. 'You've seen him, then?'

'Yes – his housemaster was troubled because the boy was sleeping badly. I saw him soon after the Easter holidays, and when I realised what was troubling him I asked him if he would like to think about sitting for the Arnold.'

Claire was nonplussed. 'What is the Arnold?' she asked.

'A scholarship, financed by an old boy – Sir Clement Arnold,' the Head explained. 'There are three places allotted each year. They sit the examination at the end of this half and the results come through about the middle of August. It's my opinion that Michael would stand a good chance, and I told him so.' He looked up. 'I'm very surprised he hasn't mentioned it to you.'

But Claire wasn't – not at all. She thought now that she understood the reason for her brother's unhappiness. Normally he would find the scholarship a stimulating challenge, but in these circumstances he would find the prospect too daunting. Too much depended upon it, and if he were to fail he would feel it keenly. She thanked the Headmaster and left, promising to discuss the matter with her mother when she got home.

But all the way back to Kingsmere on the train the problem spun round and round in her brain and only seemed to increase; snowball-like, in size. Before she left Mike she had told him to stop worrying – tried to reassure him that now that she was qualified and her mother was working again the fees weren't a problem. She hadn't told him she was seeing the Head, and now she realised that she could not let him know that she knew about the scholarship. If Mike realised she knew he might feel compelled to sit for it.

As she let herself into the flat she had almost made up her mind to discuss the whole thing with her mother, but just as she was closing the door the telephone began to ring. She picked up the receiver.

'Hello. Kingsmere 81–' She was interrupted by her mother's voice:

'Oh, Claire! I've been trying to get you for the past hour.'

'I stayed on a while at St Crispin's. Mike–' But Rosemary hurried on:

'I'll hear all about it when I get home, darling, but I'm in a kiosk and I haven't any more change so I must tell you why I'm ringing. I have to stay over tonight in London. Dav – Dr Phillips is wanted for an extra session this evening and he's agreed to stay on. He said I could come home, but I know he'd appreciate it if I stayed. There's plenty for me to do and I–' The pips began to bleep and she broke off. 'Oh, you will be all right, won't you?'

'Yes.'

'And Mike – how was he?'

But the line went dead before Claire could tell her. She replaced the receiver slowly.

Perhaps it was as well her mother wouldn't be home tonight; it would do her good to get right away in different surroundings for a while. She had sounded happier than Claire had heard her for ages – almost *excited*, she reflected with surprise. Resignedly she took off her outdoor things and prepared to make herself a meal, her heart suddenly heavy at the prospect of a lonely evening racking her brain to find a solution to Mike's problem. Why was it, she wondered, that however hard she tried there always seemed to be a shadow looming over her?

On the evening the ophthalmic unit closed its doors to allow the builders to move in, there was an informal party in the Nurses' Home common room at Queen Eleanor's. Most people concerned with the unit came, including Mr Fairbrother, who brought an enormous gateau as his contribution. Sister Baker was going over to St Winifred's temporarily, as was the other staff nurse, but most of the nursing staff were to be absorbed into other wards at Queen Eleanor's until the opening of the new, larger unit, and it seemed that Claire was the only nurse who was actually moving out to a private job. Sister Jennings, from the men's ward, was leaving anyway to have a baby. Claire was talking to her when she noticed Simon arrive. He accepted a drink and wandered over to congratulate Sister Jennings. When she moved away to talk to someone else he smiled at Claire.

'When are you planning to take up your job at Fritcham-on-Sea?' he asked.

'I'm moving this weekend,' Claire told him.

'I daresay you'll have quite a bit of luggage. I'll drive you over if you like.'

She smiled. 'That would be nice.'

'I thought we might have lunch on the way – unless you have any other plans?'

'No, none.'

He leaned close to look into her eyes. 'Anything the matter? You look a little peaky. Not worrying about the new job, are you?'

She shook her head. 'No. It's a wrench, of course, leaving here so soon after I've qualified.'

'It's only for a few weeks.' He reached out a hand to tilt her chin. 'Something else on your mind?'

She hesitated. 'Yes, there is, as a matter of fact.' Someone muttered an apology, squeez-

188

ing between them, and Claire gave him a helpless look. 'It's getting rather crowded in here.'

'Would you like to leave?' She nodded and he took her empty glass from her, dumping it, along with his own, on a side table, then taking her arm, he steered her towards the door. Outside the air was fresh and cool. He looked down at her, one eyebrow raised. 'A drink – somewhere quiet?'

'I feel guilty, taking you away from the party,' she began, but he shook his head, walking her towards the car park.

'I hate crowded rooms where you have to shout to make yourself heard,' he told her. 'Besides, I haven't seen you since the night we had dinner together.'

She knew he had been over to St Winifred's, inspecting the facilities they would have there and liaising with the Hospital Administrator. There was a lot of work connected with the temporary move.

When they were settled in a quiet corner of a small pub quite close to the hospital Simon glanced at her. 'Go ahead if you want to talk.'

She was about to begin when a thought struck her. 'I really don't know why you should be involved in all my family problems. It isn't fair.'

He looked at her levelly. 'Why not let me be the judge of that? If it's anything I can help with – or advise you on. If I didn't want to know, I wouldn't ask!'

'Well–' Claire looked down at her hands. 'It's Mike. It was his Speech Day a few days ago, and I went alone because my mother was working. Mike is unhappy. His work is suffering and he's talking about leaving. He's convinced that his school fees are making us hard up. I tried to assure him that we're all right. I even saw his Headmaster while I was there.'

'What did he say?'

'That he believes Mike is going through a period of delayed shock over losing Dad. He offered to let him try for a scholarship. There are three places to be won each year.'

'Sounds good. So what's the problem?' asked Simon.

Claire shook her head. 'I'm not sure that I know, except that Mike seems to have lost all his confidence. He didn't even tell me about the scholarship himself, which seems to point to the fact that he's afraid of sitting for it in case he fails. He kept on about letting us down – insisting that it might all be a waste of money.'

Simon smiled sympathetically. 'Poor little devil! I know how he feels. It's hard to have to grow up at thirteen – to start facing responsibility, not only for yourself but for others.'

Claire twisted the stem of her glass. 'I don't know what to do. If I tell Mum she'll only worry. As for Mike himself–'

'Let him make his own decision,' Simon advised firmly. 'He'll have to anyway if it's a case of sitting for this scholarship. No one can decide about that but him. Let him work it out, Claire.' He looked at her doubtful expression. 'Believe me, I do know what I'm talking about. I had to make my own decision when it came to a career. I had no one to advise me, no mother or father I could talk things over with. It all had to come from within – from my own instincts. I had to learn to have faith in myself, and that's not a bad thing.' He smiled wryly. 'I like to think I didn't make too much of a hash of it!'

Claire remembered his implying that he had never had a home of his own, and once more she was grateful for her own warm family background. Both she and Mike had never been without someone caring to talk to – it meant a lot to have someone who was always on your side. The rejection of the wealthy, spoiled Sally must have hurt him too – probably more deeply than he would ever admit. With a sudden rush of tenderness she reached out her hand for his. He took it, holding it firmly and warmly in his, and for a long moment they looked into each other's eyes. Simon broke the silence, saying:

'Shall we go?' She nodded and they went out to the car. As she watched him settle himself beside her, her heart swelled with love for him. Suddenly she longed to make him a real home; to be his family, to have his children. The powerful intensity of her feelings shocked her and she felt her face suffused with warm colour as she sat there in the darkness of the car.

It was only a short drive to the flat and when he drew up outside she turned to him, her eyes shining.

'Simon, thanks for your advice. I'll do as you suggest and try to let Mike work things out for himself.'

He smiled. 'Good. I'll pick you up at about eleven-thirty tomorrow, and I hope to see that worried look gone by then.' He reached out to touch her cheek, drawing her gently to him.

As she moved closer to him, smelt the faint tang of his after-shave and felt the roughness of his tweed jacket against her cheek, her pulses quickened. She lifted her face eagerly for his kiss, her lips parting beneath his and her fingers lacing into the thick hair at the nape of his neck. Her heart pounded as she strained close to him and she could hear the blood singing in her ears as she murmured:

'Oh, Simon darling, I'll make it all up to you. What you said about having no family made me feel so–' she had been about to say 'sorry', but she stopped herself, turning it to, 'hurt for you.'

In the dim light of the car she looked up at him, waiting for him to kiss her again. He did not. His eyes were dark and she felt him tense as he took her arms from around his neck and put her firmly from him.

'I'm sorry if I gave you the wrong impression, Claire,' he said coldly. 'I wasn't trying to play on your sympathy. I hope I haven't given you that impression. In many ways I suppose I've had a more privileged background than most.'

She felt herself burning with embarrassment. 'Oh, but I wasn't – you didn't – it was just what you said about having no parents–' But Simon was already getting out of the car, coming round to her side and helping her out. Cupping her elbow, he walked her firmly to the door.

'I didn't say I had no parents,' he corrected. 'I said I had no parents I could *talk* to. It isn't quite the same thing.' He looked coolly down at her. 'I'll see you at about eleven-thirty tomorrow, then.'

'Yes – thank you. Good night.'

'Good night.' Without another word he walked back to the car.

Hurriedly, Claire let herself in and stood with her back against the door, biting her lip in anguish as she listened to the sound of the car receding on the still night air. Why, oh, *why* had she allowed herself to get so carried away? She had made a complete and utter fool of herself! Not only that, but in some inexplicable way she had wounded Simon's pride. She blushed hotly as she repeated to herself the things she had said to him. She must have sounded like some starry-eyed teenager with a crush. How on earth was she going to face him tomorrow?

CHAPTER TEN

After a sleepless night Claire was up early. Moving about the flat quietly so as not to wake her mother, she packed the rest of her things, then went to the kitchen to make herself a cup of tea. It was no good, she simply could not face the thought of being driven to Fritcham with Simon – of having lunch with him after what had happened last night. Tossing and turning during the small hours, she had tried to make sense of his attitude. Was it that she had annoyed him by thinking he was a poor boy who had made good? Or could it have been her eager response to his kisses that had caused his backing off? Did he feel that she had read too much into his ardour? After all, he had never actually said that he loved her.

As she sat at the table, stirring her tea, she wished fervently that she had her own transport and could go to Fritcham under her own steam. The buses were few and far between, and she didn't relish humping her suitcases all the way into town to the bus station and then making the two-mile walk with them to Pilgrim's House. Suddenly she thought of Steve. He would take her – if he were free, that was. On impulse she went into the living room, picked up the telephone and dialled Steve's number.

It was some time before he answered, and by the sound of his voice the telephone had wakened him.

'Hello – Queen Eleanor's Home for Wayward Girls.'

Claire couldn't help smiling. Even at this time of the morning Steve couldn't resist sharpening his wits! 'Steve, it's me – Claire,' she said.

'Claire! What's the matter?' His voice was fully alert now. 'Have the Martians landed, or have you realised that you can't live without me after all?'

'I was rather hoping you'd be in a helpful mood,' she said.

'I am, I am!' he assured her. 'Just say the word. Your wish is my command.'

'Are you busy today?'

'I shall cancel everything,' he told her. 'The invitation to shoot at Sandringham, tea with the Queen, the–'

'Steve, I'm serious!' she interrupted. 'I need your help – a favour, if you like.'

'Of course, love. What do you want?' His voice softened. 'You know I'd do anything for you.'

'Well, I'm moving to Fritcham today to start my new job,' she told him. 'It's rather an awkward place to get to and I really could do with a lift. I'll pay for the petrol, of course.'

'How dare you question my chivalry? Pay for the petrol? What do you take me for, girl? What time shall I pick you up?'

She glanced at her watch. 'Well, I don't need to be there until this afternoon really–' she bit her lip, wanting to be away before Simon called for her.

'A bite of lunch on the way, then. How does that sound?' Steve asked cheerfully. 'I'll call for you about half-ten and we can make a leisurely drive of it – go the pretty way.'

'Thanks a lot, Steve,' she said gratefully.

'Not at all. I owe you a favour, if you can call it that. See you later then.'

As she replaced the receiver Claire looked again at her watch. It was still only half past seven. She still had three hours and very little to do with them. Suddenly she made up her mind. Her mother would be on her own after today, at least for the next few weeks. She would make her breakfast and take it to her in bed as a special treat.

Rosemary woke as her daughter drew back the curtains, letting in the bright sunshine. She sat up in bed and stared with delight at the loaded tray Claire put in front of her.

'What's this? It isn't my birthday!'

Claire sat down on the end of the bed. 'I shan't be here to do it for you after today – not for a while. I thought it would be nice.'

'It *is*.' Rosemary looked round the tray at the array of dishes. 'Cereal, bacon and eggs, toast and marmalade and a pot of tea.' She picked up the tiny vase Claire had added, containing two tulips. 'Even flowers! You're spoiling me.'

'I picked them from the windowbox,' Claire confessed. 'You can't have a breakfast tray without flowers, can you?'

Rosemary began to tuck in. 'Have you had yours?'

Claire nodded. 'I had it earlier – I've been up some time.'

'Excited about the new job?'

'You could say that.' Claire smoothed the quilt, trying to find the words to express what she wanted to ask. 'Mum – later, when you've had breakfast, would you make a

198

telephone call for me?'

Her mother looked up. 'Why can't you make it yourself, dear?'

'It's – awkward. You see, Simon Bonham was going to drive me over to Fritcham, but I've been thinking about it and I'd rather he didn't. I've just rung Steve to ask him to take me and he says he will.'

Her mother laid down her spoon. 'Oh, Claire, that really does sound rather ungrateful! I'm not surprised you don't want to ring him yourself. Why don't you want him to take you?'

Claire bit her lip. 'I – feel he's done enough for us already,' she hedged.

Rosemary shook her head. 'You're so independent, child. Do you think it's wise, though, asking Dr Lang to take you? Give that young man an inch and he takes a mile!'

'I can handle him,' Claire assured her. 'Anyway, he owes me a favour. Remember that fiasco about the engagement?'

Rosemary shook her head. 'That's just what I was thinking about!' She shrugged. 'Well, I suppose you know what you're doing. Just tell me what you want me to say to Mr Bonham and I'll ring him as soon as I've finished this.'

Simon had been remarkably casual when

Rosemary had rung him; it was almost as though he had been expecting the call. He hadn't even enquired how Claire was getting to Fritcham, which came as a relief to her. She hadn't primed her mother on this point and, knowing her, she would never have been able to make up something convincing on the spur of the moment. Steve had called for her on the dot often, and after kissing her mother goodbye she had run down to meet him, helping to pack her cases into the boot of his car. At last she was on her way, and as the car drew away from the kerb she wound down the car window to wave to her mother.

Steve drove through the winding, wooded roads – 'the pretty way', as he called it. They stopped for a ploughman's lunch at a tiny pub on the way, and as they strolled back to the car afterwards Steve looked at Claire.

'Still plenty of time. How about a walk through the woods?'

She shrugged. 'All right. I don't want to get there until Miss Lattimer has finished her lunch.'

As they walked through the pinewoods, Steve flung an arm carelessly across her shoulders. 'Tell me, what made you call me so suddenly this morning?' he asked. 'It's not like you to have overlooked a little thing like how you were going to get there.'

She took a deep breath. 'I was getting a lift,' she told him, 'but it fell through.'

He looked down at her, eyes narrowed. 'I see. At a guess I'd say there's more to it than that – but I shan't press you further.' He laughed. 'When you're as devious as I am you see through other people very easily, you know.'

'Or read more into their actions than you should,' she countered. 'You shouldn't judge everyone by yourself, you know, Steve.'

He stopped and swung her round to face him. 'Seriously though, whatever the reason, I was pleased you asked me. I've had cause to regret forcing you into playing that idiot trick on my mother.'

'I should hope so too!' She tried to move away, but he held her firmly.

'She really liked you, you know. When she eventually got the truth out of me she gave me the tongue-lashing of my life.'

'Serves you right!'

'She told me I didn't deserve a girl like you,' Steve went on, 'and that if I knew what was good for me I'd try to get you back before it was too late.' He drew her a little closer, looking down into her eyes. *Is* it too late, Claire?'

She began to feel uneasy. 'I don't know what you mean, Steve – there's no question of its being too late, as you put it. You know there was never anything between us – and there never could be.'

'You don't mean that!'

'I do. We've been friends for a long time, I grant you, even though there have been times when you've put even that under a severe strain. As for any other kind of relationship, it just isn't on. You know it as well as I do.' She pulled away from him and began to walk on, but he caught her up, a hand on her shoulder.

'Claire, wait! Listen to me. Lately I've been taking stock. I don't feel the way I used to. I know you were pretty disgusted with me over what I did and I agree it was stupid and childish, but it made me start thinking. I know now what I want, and it isn't all this fooling about, playing silly jokes on people.' He looked at her gravely, his freckled face serious for once. 'In other words, I've grown up, believe it or not!'

'Then what *is* it you want, Steve?' She turned to face him.

'I want you, Claire.'

She stared at him speechlessly for a

moment. It was another of his practical jokes. In a minute he'd be falling about at the shocked expression on her face. But he continued to look at her, his eyes holding a look she'd never seen in them before, and slowly the realisation that he was in deadly earnest sank in.

'Steve, you can't–' she began, but before she had time to say any more he pulled her to him and kissed her soundly.

'I love you, Claire.' He held her close. 'I've never been really in love before. I had no idea it could be like this – this awful mixture of hurt and happiness. It suddenly hit me like a ton of bricks. Look–' he held her away to look down at her, 'I know it's probably a bit hard to accept, but if you could just think about it–'

Dismay filled Claire's heart. In reality, Steve had got what he deserved, but she had always been soft-hearted and they had been friends for a long time. Instinct told her she would have to be firm. Her mother had been right – give Steve an inch and he would take a mile.

'There's no point, Steve. I could never think of you in that way.'

He looked crestfallen. 'It's Bonham, isn't it?'

'I don't want to discuss it,' she said, beginning to walk back towards the car. 'Anyway, it's irrelevant. As far as I'm concerned there's never been any possibility of that kind of relationship between you and me.' She glanced at him. 'We can still be friends, of course.'

'Oh, thanks!' he said bitterly. 'I never thought I'd hear an old cliché like that from you.'

The rest of the drive to Fritcham was spent in silence, Steve driving uncharacteristically carefully, his face as doleful as a whipped puppy's. As they drew up outside Pilgrim's House Claire opened her handbag.

'Please, Steve – let me pay for the petrol as I asked?'

He shot her a wounded look. 'What are you trying to do, emasculate me completely? Aren't you satisfied with destroying my male ego for ever?'

She tried hard not to laugh; the idea of destroying Steve's male ego was unimaginable. 'You'll find someone else, Steve,' she promised. 'You know you will.'

He shook his head, looking at her with genuine wistfulness. 'I suggest you get out of this car now – before I decide to abduct you.

I'm quite capable of it, you know.'

'I *do* know!' She got out of the car and he helped her lift her luggage out of the boot. 'Are you going to come in and meet my patient?' she asked.

He shook his head. 'No, I'll say goodbye here.' He looked at his watch. 'If I hurry I might still be in time for tea with the Queen after all!' He kissed her lightly. 'I won't give up this easily, Claire,' he said quietly. 'Not after it's taken me this long to see the light!'

Phyllis Lattimer opened the door to Claire herself. 'So you've arrived safely.' She peered out into the drive. 'But how did you get here?'

'A friend from the hospital brought me,' Claire told her. 'But he was in rather a hurry.'

'What a pity.' Phyllis closed the door and took one of Claire's cases. 'Still, never mind. Come upstairs – I daresay you'd like to freshen up before tea.'

Her room was at the back of the house, overlooking the garden. She unpacked, then went down to the drawing room where Phyllis was waiting. On the table drawn up before the fireplace was a laden tea tray, and Claire was surprised to see a large, gooey-looking chocolate gateau on it. She looked at her patient.

'Surely you don't eat that?'

Phyllis smiled. 'No, that's for you, my dear. Mrs Winters made it specially. I think she enjoyed doing it – I'm afraid she sometimes finds cooking for me rather boring. All I'm allowed with my tea is two biscuits.' She sat down and began to pour. 'I don't mind as much as I used to. There's a bonus, you see: I don't have to worry about putting on weight like I once did.'

'How long have you been diabetic?' asked Claire.

'About twenty years altogether.' Phyllis cut a generous slice of gateau and handed it to Claire. 'My first worry was that my son might inherit it, but I was soon reassured on that count. I believe the statistics are about one and a half per cent, and as he's over thirty now there seems little chance of his contracting it.'

'What treatment are you on?' asked Claire. 'What's your routine?'

'I'm on Isophane insulin now,' Phyllis told her. 'As I expect you know, it has an extended action. I take blood tests with the help of one of the new Diatrons. When I was doing a lot of travelling, especially where time changes were involved, I used to run into trouble,' she explained. 'I don't have the same problems now, of course, but I still find this way the most convenient.'

'You have a Diatron? I haven't actually seen one yet,' Claire told her. 'Though I've heard they're a great improvement on the old method of testing.'

'They are. Small enough to fit into your pocket or handbag and so much more reliable than comparing colours on a chart, especially in artificial light.' Phyllis poured herself another cup of tea. 'One big problem I used to face was my nerves just before a concert.'

'How do you mean?' asked Claire.

'Adrenalin. The sudden rush of adrenalin one gets with nervous anxiety produces the same effect as a hypo. In the beginning I was in constant fear that I might be going into one during a concert.'

'It can't have been easy for you,' Claire said sympathetically.

Phyllis shook her head: 'Developing retinopathy was the last straw. That was when I finally decided to call it a day, though I'd been easing up over the years.'

'You must miss it – all the excitement, the travelling and so on.'

The older woman shook her head. 'Not

really. There comes a time when we all feel the need to slow down.' She smiled wryly. 'And you know, although I've travelled all over the world I've never really seen the places I visited. I was always too busy rehearsing. I never saw much more than the airports, the concert halls and the hotels I stayed in.'

After tea Claire watched while her patient took the second of the day's routine blood tests. She had offered to do it for her, but Phyllis shook her head, laughing. 'If you'll forgive me, my dear, I daresay I've taken more of these than you have in your entire career. Supervise, by all means, and perhaps on days when I'm not feeling so well – maybe after my op – I shall be glad to have someone to do it for me. But for now I think I might as well carry on as always, don't you?'

Claire watched as she washed and dried her hands carefully, then used a small Manolet lancet to prick her fingertip, catching the droplet of blood on the end of the test strip. Phyllis showed her the digital read-out on the small, compact Diatron machine, then marked it carefully on the chart she kept. Claire glanced at the chart and saw that the blood-glucose levels seemed to be maintaining a steady, smoothed-out rhythm.

'You seem to have things well under control,' she said, smiling. 'I think you were right when you said I would learn a lot from being with you. When are you expecting to have your operation?'

'Quite soon. Next week, in fact,' Phyllis told her. 'I'm going into a private clinic in London, but as I have you to look after me I shall be allowed home almost immediately.' She smiled. 'I'm glad. I hate being in hospital!'

'While you are in you'll find that the nurses will insist on giving you your injections,' warned Claire. 'It's the rule under the General Nursing Council's insurance.'

'Oh, I understand that,' said Phyllis with a twinkling smile. 'I'm quite a reasonable person really.'

Claire went upstairs after tea to finish her unpacking and change. She had asked whether there was anything she could do to help in the kitchen, but Phyllis had assured her that Mrs Winters had left a chicken casserole in the oven for dinner and everything was under control.

'I forgot to tell you, my son will be joining us for dinner,' Phyllis told her. 'I thought it would be nice for you to meet.'

Claire chose a simple dark grey dress to wear for dinner, with a wide black patent belt and sandals to match. She thought she heard a car draw up while she was putting the final touches to her hair, then the sound of the door being opened and voices in the hall below. She wondered what Phyllis's son would be like as she went down the curving staircase. Voices were coming from the drawing room and she cleared her throat as she opened the door, hoping she was not intruding on a private conversation. As she entered the room Phyllis looked up.

'Ah, there you are, my dear. Will you have a sherry? I hope you like dry – that's all I'm allowed.' She poured a glass and came towards Claire with it. 'I'd like you to meet my son. I told you we would have a guest for dinner.'

The tall man standing by the fireplace turned and Claire caught her breath in surprise. Phyllis smiled at him proudly.

'Simon, come and meet Claire Simms, my new nurse. Or perhaps you've already met. Isn't it a coincidence, the two of you working in the same hospital?'

CHAPTER ELEVEN

As Phyllis hurried off again to the kitchen Claire stared at Simon. 'Why didn't you tell me – or your mother?' she asked in a whisper.

He smiled coolly, gently swirling the contents of his glass. 'You seemed determined to get the job off your own bat, so I decided to let you.'

'But you'll tell her now?' she said. 'At least we'd better have the same story, otherwise the conversation could get very difficult.'

'She's under the impression that I put an advertisement in one of the nursing journals,' he told her. 'As a matter of fact that was exactly what I intended to do. I simply decided to give you first refusal of the job.'

She looked at him. 'Why me?' she asked him. 'There have been times when you've criticised my attitude to nursing – yet you trust me with your own mother!'

The smile left his face and he walked over to the window, looking out into the garden. 'You have heart,' he said at last. 'Maybe a little too much for a nurse. You still have to learn to control it, but nevertheless–'

His analytical attitude irritated her. 'I see! It's different when you find yourself facing the other side of the coin, though, isn't it?' she flung at him triumphantly.

Simon swung round to face her, his eyes angry. 'It isn't like that! My mother is – vulnerable. She doesn't have anyone. I'd like her to have the best–' he frowned and shook his head impatiently – 'the most *suitable* nurse at this time.'

'I take it that's a compliment?' Claire said crisply.

He shrugged. 'You must take it in whatever way you choose. It's a professional opinion, for what it's worth.'

She was fighting down the tight knot of tears in her throat by now as she said: 'I thought you had something more than just a professional opinion of me!'

A shadow crossed his brow and he took a step towards her. 'Claire, I–' But at that moment the door opened and Phyllis came in.

'You two been having a nice chat? Good. Now where did I put my drink? Everything's ready, so we can go into the dining room if you like.'

Over the meal Claire's mind was working fast. There was something very strange about the whole set-up. Why had Simon said that his mother had no one when she had him? She remembered the things Phyllis had said about her son on that first day: 'I don't think he's ever quite forgiven me for not making a secure home for him.'– 'There was a girl once – a lovely girl.'– 'Sometimes I feel that the women in his life have given him a rather poor view of the opposite sex!'

'Claire dear, is everything all right? You're not eating a thing!'

Claire looked up, startled from her preoccupation by Phyllis's anxious voice. 'Oh, I'm just a slow eater, that's all. It's delicious.' She lowered her eyes and began to apply herself to the food before her. So much was now becoming clear to her. Sally, the girl in the photograph, must be the 'lovely girl' Phyllis had spoken of. The one Simon had been so much in love with. Clearly, when he had spoken of her he had deliberately played the affair down. And what was his relationship with his mother now? she wondered. Did he feel guilty? Since he had become a mature man perhaps he had come to realise that people didn't

213

always have full control over their lives – that gifted people sometimes have to make intolerable sacrifices that are difficult for lesser mortals particularly family, to understand. Was he using her, Claire, to do what he couldn't do himself – to give love and support to his mother in her time of need?

She realised suddenly that Simon and his mother were talking about the operation, to take place next Thursday. Simon sounded impatient.

'I've told you, it's far better to have the operations one at a time, see how it goes. Anyway, your left eye is hardly affected at all at the moment.'

As Phyllis reached for her coffee cup Claire noticed how she turned her head to see where it was, and realised for the first time that the sight in her right eye was quite severely diminished. It was clear that she had learned to manage well, but without the operation she would soon lose the sight of it completely.

'Is a London consultant doing your operation?' she asked.

Phyllis turned to look at her. 'Yes, in his small private clinic. He's Simon's old professor, James Darnley.'

'That's interesting. I've heard of him, of

course,' Claire told her. 'How are you travelling?'

'I shall be driving her up,' Simon put in. 'I hope you will accompany us.'

'Of course – that's what I'm here for!' Too late, Claire realised that her tone was a little too sharp and she saw Phyllis's puzzled look as she glanced from one to the other of them. Simon said quickly:

'I'm sure Professor Darnley will be happy for you to watch the operation from his observation gallery. He's doing a vitrectomy. You won't have seen micro-surgery before, so I'm sure you'll find it interesting.'

'I will.' Claire took a sip of her coffee. 'He's not using photo-coagulation, then?' She had been reading up on retinopathy and had quite expected the more revolutionary method from a Harley Street man.

Simon shook his head. 'No. He feels that the vitrectomy would be more suitable in Phyllis's case.'

Somewhere in the back of her mind she registered the fact that he didn't use the word 'mother'. 'But micro-surgery takes so long, I was wondering about the anaesthetic–'

'I'm having it done under a local,' Phyllis told her triumphantly. 'And when it's all over I intend to write an article about it for the BDA magazine, to encourage others who are afraid of the operation.'

'That's very brave of you,' said Claire.

The older woman shook her head. 'Not really. It just gives me something to take my mind off the whole thing. While it's being done I shall be so busy trying to take note of what's going on that I shan't think about myself, you see.'

As they rose from the table Claire enquired about the washing-up, but was told that the dishes would all go into the automatic dishwasher. Phyllis insisted on dealing with them unaided, and as she wheeled the loaded trolley away towards the kitchen Claire looked at Simon.

'She's very independent.'

'It's just as well,' he said. 'It wouldn't do to be totally dependent on others in her position, would it?'

He sounded so cool and detached, Claire thought he might have been speaking about a complete stranger instead of his own mother. 'The vitrectomy,' she said. 'What are the chances of success?'

'Good,' he replied. 'Darnley is the best man in the country – in Europe perhaps, and we've caught it in time. There's no sign of retinal detachment as yet.'

'And will she really be able to write that article?'

He smiled wryly. 'I think you know the answer to that. As far as the anaesthetic is concerned, she'll be so heavily sedated that she probably won't remember much afterwards, and what she does will be wildly inaccurate. But we won't say anything about that for the time being.'

'Simon—' she looked at him tentatively, 'the other night – I said something that annoyed you. I still don't know what it was, but–'

He silenced her with a look. 'It was nothing – forget it. There are some subjects on which I'm touchy, that's all – my childhood is one of them.'

'I only meant–'

'Look, Claire–' he leaned towards her, 'perhaps I made a mistake, involving myself in your life. I should have taken more notice when you told me to stop interfering. For a long time I fought off the attraction I felt for you. I think you sensed that. I should have obeyed my first instincts. They're usually right, don't you agree?'

She stared at him, shaking her head dumbly. She hadn't the slightest idea what he was talking about.

'If I've caused you any – any trouble or inconvenience, I'm sorry,' he went on. 'And I hope that the temporary job here, nursing Phyllis, will make up for it in some small way.' His eyes slid away from hers as he rose from the table and went to open the door. 'I'm grateful to you for taking it,' he said as she passed in front of him through the door he held open. 'I'm confident that she'll be happy and safe in your care, and I hope that the salary will help with your own family problems.'

Claire turned to look at him, her eyes dark with hurt. 'You make it all sound so clinical,' she said accusingly. 'So calculated and cold – like a business arrangement!'

'Well, isn't it?' He turned to look at her.

'Before dinner you were talking about "heart",' she reminded him.

He gave a dry little laugh. 'And one of the coldest facts of life is that the more money you have, the more "heart" you can buy! It seems to apply in every kind of human relationship you can think of.'

She stared at him, shocked to the core at his cynicism, but before she could think of a suitable reply Phyllis came into the hall.

'Good heavens, what are you two doing, standing about out here? Let's go into the drawing room. I've got some of your favourite brandy, Simon.'

He shook his head. 'I've got to go – there's a patient I want to look in on. I'll see you on Wednesday. Good night.' He looked at her. 'Good night, Claire.' She searched his eyes for the slightest flicker of regret – of veiled wistfulness – but they stared back at her, their intense blue gaze telling her nothing. A moment later he was gone.

Life at Pilgrim's House was easy and Claire settled in well over the few days that followed. Indeed she felt superfluous – more like a guest than an employee. Phyllis insisted on doing her own tests and injections. She managed her diabetes perfectly, and Claire felt a little ashamed to find herself looking forward to her return from the clinic when she would have a patient to nurse once again.

Simon did not appear at the house again, though Phyllis talked about him often. She was obviously proud of her son and his achievements, trying desperately hard to make up for the time they had lost together when he was younger, and Claire's heart ached for her as she remembered his coldness.

On Wednesday afternoon the familiar silver-grey saloon drew up outside. Claire saw it from the open front door where she was just depositing Phyllis's case, along with her own. They would be staying in London for only a couple of days, yet Phyllis seemed to be taking almost the entire contents of her bedroom.

'I like to feel at home,' she explained.

Simon was silent on the journey, but Phyllis made up for it. Claire could not make up her mind whether it was nerves or excitement making her so garrulous.

When Phyllis was settled in her room at the clinic, surrounded by her photographs and knicknacks, Simon took Claire along to the small hotel nearby where they were booked in. He waited while she signed the register, then asked:

'What are you going to do with yourself this evening?'

'I shall go and sit with your mother for a while,' she told him. 'Unless you intended to stay with her, of course.'

'No. I'm seeing Professor Darnley later,' he told her. 'But I understand that he won't be free until after six.' He hesitated. 'I thought perhaps we could have a meal first?'

She felt her cheeks colour hotly. 'Please

don't feel you have to entertain me! Or, perhaps you have nothing better to do?'

He sighed. 'Oh dear, I was afraid I'd upset you. I'd like a chance to explain some of the things I said the other night, Claire. If you don't eat with me you'll have several hours to lose, so you might as well accept my offer.' He smiled ruefully. 'Surely it's better than being bored?'

She accepted somewhat ungraciously, despising the traitorous quickening of her heartbeat as she went off to her room to change.

Simon waited for her in the hotel lounge and she rejoined him half an hour later, wearing the only other outfit she had brought with her, a dark green velvet suit with a plain white silk shirt.

The restaurant he chose was tucked away in a quiet street, on the far side of a court-yard. The spring evening was warm and mellow, and diners sat drinking aperitifs at tables with brightly coloured umbrellas that had been set out on the cobblestones. As a waiter showed them to a table for two, Simon looked at her.

'Have you settled in? Do you like it at Pilgrim's House? I haven't had a chance to ask you yet.'

'I'm fine, thank you,' Claire said stiffly.

He reached across to touch her hand.

'I do care, you know,' he said quietly. 'I'm not just asking to be polite.'

She did not reply, burying her head in the menu. When they had ordered, he looked at her.

'You seem to get along well with Phyllis?'

'Of course. Your mother is a very nice person,' she replied stiffly.

'Do I detect a reproach?' he asked wryly.

Claire blushed. 'You said you wanted to say something – about your behaviour the other evening.'

'I apologise.' Simon held her gaze, pausing as the waiter put their food before them. 'I admit that I was annoyed at your telephone message – especially when I learned later that you'd asked Lang to take you to Fritcham.'

She picked up her knife and fork, bending her head in the hope that he wouldn't see the flush that rose to her cheeks. Steve had certainly lost no time in spreading the word. What was it he had said? 'I don't give up as easily as that.'

'I thought that in the circumstances it might be better,' she said. 'I had no idea then that Phyllis was your mother. You can hardly blame me for that. And I asked Steve because I knew he'd–'

'Jump at the chance to score over me?' Simon supplied. 'Even if the victory is entirely in his own mind.'

Claire flushed. 'The thought never entered my head – and I'm sure it didn't occur to him either,' she added with more vehemence than conviction. 'But if reproaches are the order of the day, I might as well say that I think you could make an effort to be kinder to your mother. She obviously adores you, and she'll never need you more than she does at the moment. You told me yourself that she was vulnerable.' He was silent and for a moment she wondered if she had gone too far, then he said slowly:

'It isn't easy to explain to you – a person from a normal family background. All her life, until now, Phyllis has been totally self-sufficient – needed nothing but her music. There were times during my childhood, and when I was growing up, that I badly needed her. She was never there – always off on some concert tour. I was an only child and my father left when I was still too young to know him – again the result of her voracious career.' He looked at her with clouded eyes. 'I know how it feels to be alone. I learned to rely on myself over the years, I had a good teacher, she can hardly complain if I learned that lesson well!'

Simon's feelings obviously went deep and Claire felt she had intruded on something very private. 'It's none of my business,' she said quietly. 'Who am I to judge?'

'I can see how it must look to you,' he said. 'But try to understand. I'm doing now what she has always done – my duty. I can't do more or less. It's too late.'

'I see.' Claire looked at him, wondering how this man who could be so kind and caring to his patients could feel so little for his own mother. The memory of the evening she had spent with him in his house rose to her mind, the warmth of his arms around her, the hungry need of his lips on hers. Was all that simply physical attraction? Had he felt no more than the basic biological need of a man for a woman? Was he *really* so cold? She looked at him with new eyes, remembering his words at dinner the other evening: 'I made a mistake, involving myself in your life.' So detached. He might have been cancelling a theatre booking or a dental appointment.

'Thank you for telling me how you feel,' she said. Her voice was calm, though inside her heart was throbbing with a dull ache. All she wanted to do was to get away from the restaurant, back to her hotel room where she could close the door and give way to the tears. 'I think we've both been wrong about each other. You were right – it's as well to discover these things in time.'

The Marie Fry Clinic was named for Professor Darnley's wife and was equipped with every comfort for its twenty patients. Claire was there bright and early next morning and looked in on her patient as she was being prepared for her operation. Phyllis seemed pleased to see her.

'Good morning, dear. Did you sleep well? Are they making you comfortable at the hotel?'

Claire nodded. She had slept hardly at all, but it wouldn't do to let her patient see how weary and depressed she felt. 'I'm fine. How about you?'

'I had a very good night. I believe they slipped something into my bedtime drink.' She chuckled. 'You were right about not being allowed to do my own injection,' she said. 'But Professor Darnley came to see me last night and he explained about it.' She sighed. 'He's so nice, so calm and under-standing. He inspires confidence in one at

225

once, and I think that's so important in a doctor, don't you?'

Claire agreed. 'I've enquired, and it seems that you're second on the list.' She looked at her watch. 'That means you'll be going off to the theatre in about an hour. The Professor likes to make an early start. A nurse will be along shortly to instill some drops, then when you go to the theatre you'll have some little injections around the eye. You needn't worry, you won't feel a thing.'

'Oh, I'm not worried, dear. I know I'm in good hands. Simon saw to all that for me.' Phyllis chatted for a while, but soon the sedative the nurse had given her began to work and her concentration began to slip. She looked at Claire.

'Oh dear, I feel sleepy. I hope I'm not going to miss anything.'

Claire squeezed her hand. 'Not you. Why not snatch forty winks now, before they come to collect you?'

Phyllis sighed. 'Do you know, my dear, I think I will. You are going to be there, aren't you?' Her fingers curled tightly round Claire's.

'Of course,' she promised.

Outside in the corridor a thick fitted

carpet muffled her footsteps as she made her way towards the waiting room. She didn't hear anyone behind her and jumped in surprise when a quiet voice addressed her.

'Claire, if you like I'll show you the way to the observation gallery. I've asked permission for you to watch the operation from there.'

Her heart somersaulted at his sudden appearance. She had planned to avoid him today. 'Have you been in to see your mother?' she asked.

'I looked in just now, but she was asleep,' he told her. 'If you'd like to come with me—'

She hung back. 'If you could just tell me how to find it. I've promised to be with her when they come for her, you see,' she told him.

He shrugged, his eyes cool. 'As you wish.'

Claire was sitting by Phyllis's bed when the porters came to take her to the theatre. She was transferred gently to the trolley and Claire walked with her as far as the lift. As they waited Claire took her hand and smiled down at her.

'I'll be watching all the time,' she said, adding: 'And so will Simon.'

She slipped quietly into the gallery with its

glass wall overlooking the theatre, sitting at the end of a row. Looking round, she saw that it was equipped with closed-circuit television, so that close-ups of the intricate surgery could be viewed on monitors at either end of the gallery. Most of the seats were filled, mainly by young men, students, she guessed, from the eye hospital close by. Below them, the theatre was being prepared by the Theatre Sister and scrub nurse, and Claire watched as they laid out instruments, counting and noting them carefully. Much of the equipment was strange to her. Above the operating plinth, suspended periscope-fashion, was the ophthalmic microscope.

'The Professor will be using special micro-scissors.' She looked up as Simon slipped into the seat next to hers. 'The blades are a fraction of an inch long and operated by compressed air, worked by foot controls.' He peered down into the theatre. 'I only wish we had half this technology available to us at Queen Eleanor's.'

She looked at him. 'You might like to know that your mother went off to the theatre in good spirits,' she said pointedly.

Her cool gaze was returned steadily. 'I'm glad. Though she may not be quite so pleased when she realises she won't be able to see anything,' he told her. 'The local anaesthetic will obliterate all sight from the eye being operated on and they'll cover the other one. In any case, she'll be so heavily sedated that she probably won't remember a thing.'

'She's going to be terribly disappointed,' said Claire, taking a notebook and pencil out of her handbag. 'That's one of the reasons I'm going to take notes. Between us we'll get that article written!'

Silence fell as Professor Darnley entered the theatre. Gloved hands held up, he addressed his team cheerfully:

'A vitrectomy is next on the list this morning, ladies and gentlemen, to be performed under local anaesthetic on a patient suffering from diabetic retinopathy.' He turned to his anaesthetist. 'Not much work for you to do this time, Dr Fraser,' he said jovially.

As the patient was wheeled in the Professor addressed the surgical team and onlookers: 'Retinopathy is a progressive disease, related to diabetes. Over the years new and abnormal blood vessels have formed on the retina, eventually bleeding into the vitreous. The subsequent clots have affected the patient's sight. Fortunately, in this case the condition has been diagnosed before detachment had occurred. I shall remove the damaged vitreous and replace it.'

Sterile cloths were applied and the scrub nurse moved in with her trolley of instruments. Professor Darnley made himself comfortable on the adjustable stool by the plinth. Simon touched Claire's arm.

'He works in that position to allow him to work the foot pedals that control the hydraulic instruments,' he explained to her. 'See the binocular microscope? It magnifies fifty times, and its lenses are operated by foot controls too.'

As they watched all animosity between them was forgotten in the fascination of the surgeon's skill. They saw, with the aid of the television monitors, the damaged vitreous being removed with a tiny instrument no larger than a pencil, which poured a steady light on to the operation site. Claire noted that it could cut, suction and inject, saving the surgeon having to change from one instrument to another for the different functions. Her pencil flew rapidly over the notepad. Out of the corner of his eye, Simon watched her.

'The needles used for suture are the thickness of two red blood cells,' he prompted, 'and the thread is one fourth the thickness of a human hair.'

She glanced up at him, noting the information. 'Thank you.' She was totally involved, trying hard not to miss anything that happened while jotting down all that she saw. But when it came to the suturing she laid down her pad to lean forward, fascinated by the skill needed to handle the microscopic needle, carrying almost invisible thread. Suddenly something drew her eyes to Simon, sitting motionless beside her. He hadn't spoken for several minutes. She had thought that, like her, he was fascinated by the great man's skill, but now, looking at him, she saw that his face was ashen. Reaching out, she took his hand.

'Simon?' she whispered. 'Simon, are you all right?'

His fingers gripped hers convulsively and he turned towards her for a fraction of a second, giving her just enough time to see the expression in his eyes before he released her hand and stood up, leaving the gallery without a word.

For a moment she sat motionless, wondering whether to follow him, her mind trying to analyse what she had seen in his eyes. Then the quiet voice of one of the students sitting behind her crystallised it for her.

'The patient is his mother, isn't she?' he said softly. 'I know how he must be feeling.' The young man smiled as she turned to look at him. 'It doesn't seem to matter how experienced you are when it comes to your own flesh and blood, does it?'

CHAPTER TWELVE

Claire watched as Phyllis was wheeled away to the recovery room. She heard the Professor thank his team and pronounce the operation completely satisfactory. Knowing that it would be some time before she would be allowed to see her patient, she made up her mind.

In reception she asked about Simon, and the receptionist nodded. Yes, she had seen him. He had left a few minutes ago, but had left no messages.

It took Claire only minutes to walk round the corner to the hotel. At the desk she asked the number of Simon's room and found that it was on the same floor as her own. A few minutes later she was tapping on the door. When she received no reply she took a deep breath and tried the door. It was unlocked. She pushed it open and saw Simon standing by the window, his back towards her. She began to walk towards him, but when she was a few feet away he turned. For a moment they stared at each other, then she said gently:

'Your mother's fine, Simon. Professor Darnley seemed quite happy with the result of the operation.' She took a step towards him. 'I'm sure she'd be happy to see you. Will you come with me?' She held out her hand.

For a moment he said nothing, ignoring the hand she offered, his face enigmatic, then he said huskily: 'I always *said* you had too much heart. Phyllis is your patient, damn it – not me!'

Before she could react his hands shot out to grasp her shoulders, pulling her against him and holding her close. Her throat tight, Claire said nothing more, but clung to him, sensing the need she knew he couldn't express. After a moment he released her and she looked up at him. He was himself again; completely recovered.

'Shall we go back to the clinic?' she asked quietly.

'You go,' he told her. 'I have a lunch appointment with Professor Darnley. I want to talk to him about her. I'll be looking in later.' He put her gently from him, smiling. 'Thank you, Claire.'

She hesitated. 'Shall I – give her your love?' she asked.

He nodded. 'Yes – yes, do that.'

Two days later Phyllis Lattimer was allowed home. Simon had had to return to Queen Eleanor's on the day following the operation, so a hired car had been ordered to take them back to Norfolk. Phyllis, her eye still patched, chattered excitedly most of the way. She was delighted to find that Claire had taken notes during the operation and was planning to begin writing her article the moment her dressing came off.

'I have a dinner party to organise too, dear,' she added as the leafy Hertfordshire lanes gave way to flat Cambridgeshire fen country. 'I haven't told you about that yet. Before Professor Darnley discharged me this morning he told me that he's coming to Kingsmere at the end of next week, as part of a short lecture tour. He said he'd visit me to check on the progress of my eye at the same time, to save me making the trip to London again, so naturally I invited him to come to dinner with us. I thought it was the least I could do.'

Claire smiled. 'Mrs Winters will enjoy organising that. Are you planning to ask anyone else?'

'Simon, of course, if he's free that evening,' said Phyllis. 'And the Professor will be bringing his daughter. She's going to accompany him on this tour, to work as his secretary. The poor girl has recently lost her husband and he's hoping that the work will help to give her a new interest.' She smiled. 'It will be so nice to see her again – for Simon too.'

Claire looked at her. 'Oh, you know her, then?'

Phyllis nodded eagerly. 'Oh yes. Simon and she were very close once – when he was still a student. Sally worked as a secretary at the hospital where he trained, but she married and went to America.'

Claire's heart plummeted. 'I believe you told me about her,' she said quietly.

Phyllis smiled. 'You're quite right, I believe I did.' She smiled. 'I'm not going to tell him she's back in England and coming to dinner. It's to be a surprise. I can't wait to see the look on his face when he sees her again!' She smiled coyly. 'And who knows what might come of it?' She patted Claire's hand. 'Now, my dear, the moment we get back to Fritcham you must feel free to ring your mother and arrange to drive over to Kingsmere to see her. Mrs Winters will keep me company for a couple of hours. I know how much your mother must be missing you.'

The following evening, after satisfying herself that Phyllis had everything she needed, including the company of Mrs Winters, Claire took the car and drove over to Kingsmere, having first telephoned her mother. She found a bundle of mail waiting for her at the flat, which Rosemary said she had been going to send on to her. Claire looked through the assortment of letters and postcards – three from colleagues at Queen Eleanor's who were on holiday, a couple of circulars and another long brown, official-looking envelope that puzzled her as she turned it over in her hands. While her mother slipped into the kitchen to put the kettle on for coffee she quickly slit it open. It was a notice to appear at the Crown Court in Kingsmere in a week's time as key witness in a case of attempted armed robbery at Palmer's garage. Claire was overwhelmed with dismay as she quickly stuffed the letter into her handbag along with the others. It was naive of her, but she had imagined she had heard the last of the episode. She didn't see how it could be kept out of the papers this time. She wondered if Simon had been summoned to appear too, and her heart sank. He had acted on impulse, but in the cold light of day he would surely see the whole thing as a tiresome nuisance.

In her preoccupation with the letter she failed to notice an air of suppressed excitement about her mother as she chatted over the coffee cups. They exchanged news – Claire told her mother about the operation she had witnessed at the Marie Fry Clinic and Rosemary related all the news from Queen Eleanor's.

'And your job with Dr Phillips – how is that going?' asked Claire.

Rosemary blushed, busying herself suddenly with the empty cups, her hands trembling slightly as she stacked them on to the tray. 'Actually, I have some news,' she said awkwardly. 'David and I–' she glanced at her daughter, 'we've been seeing each other socially – we've had dinner a couple of times.'

Claire smiled. 'Oh, good. That's nice of you.'

'He lost his wife some years ago, you know,' Rosemary went on. 'It's amazing how much we seem to have in common.'

Claire looked at her mother and suddenly light began to dawn. 'Are you trying to tell me he's asked you to marry him?' she said.

Rosemary looked up in surprise. 'Oh dear,

you've guessed.' She peered at her daughter anxiously. 'Do you hate the idea?'

Claire laughed. 'Hate it? I think it's super! Now that I think of it, you're perfect for each other. So when's the happy day?'

Her mother shook her head. 'Oh, it isn't quite as simple as that. There are a lot of things to be worked out before we start thinking of fixing a date.' She sighed. 'I can't tell you what a relief it is, you taking it so well.'

'But why shouldn't I?' asked Claire. 'After all, you have a life of your own to lead. You're still young.'

'Mike doesn't share your opinion, I'm afraid,' Rosemary said unhappily. 'I telephoned him last night and told him the news, and he took it rather badly.'

'Maybe you should have waited until he came home,' said Claire, wincing inwardly. 'So that they could meet each other and Mike could get used to the idea.'

'I suppose I did rather spring it on him,' Rosemary agreed. 'I was just so anxious for him to be – one of the first to hear – along with you, of course.'

Claire was worried, wishing now that she had told her mother of Mike's unsettled frame of mind. This wasn't going to help, in fact it might make matters a whole lot worse.

'David would like us all to get together as soon as possible,' her mother went on. 'He's taking me to his sister's for the weekend. We're hoping to slip away just after lunch on Friday. It isn't far from St Crispin's, and I thought we might slip over on Sunday and take Mike out to tea.' She looked at Claire hopefully. 'I suppose you couldn't join us there?'

'I'm afraid I couldn't this Sunday,' Clare told her. 'I don't like leaving Phyllis when she is so recently undergone surgery. But do go and introduce Mike to Dr Phillips,' she added quickly, seeing the disappointed look on her mother's face. 'I think that's a very good idea.'

Back at Pilgrim's House she was in time to have a bedtime drink with her patient. Phyllis chatted about Mrs Winters and her family, whose news she had been hearing during the evening.

'She has four daughters, you know – all married now.' She sighed. 'Four grand-children, and another due in a few weeks.' She looked at Claire. 'When you have a family there's always something happening, isn't there? You must know that yourself.'

'Oh, I do,' Claire smiled wryly to herself. 'Sometimes there's more happening than you can cope with!'

Phyllis leaned forward, peering at her. 'Are you all right, my dear? There's nothing wrong at home, is there? You know, they say when one's sight goes one develops a heightened perception. I can see enough to know that your pretty face is troubled, and since you came in you've been – I don't know–' she frowned, searching for the word, 'subdued.'

Claire opened her handbag and fingered the brown envelope inside. 'I – had a rather disturbing letter this evening,' she said slowly. 'It was waiting for me at the flat.'

She knew she would have to arrange for time off to go to court anyway. And she ached to confide in someone. Almost before she realised it she had regaled Phyllis with the whole story of her mother's redundancy, Mike's increased fees, her moonlighting job at Palmer's garage and the attempted robbery, foiled by Simon. The older woman listened quietly, shaking her head sympathetically from time to time.

'Now that the case is coming to court it will be bound to make the papers,' Claire finished, shaking her head despairingly.

241

'Simon did what he did on the spur of the moment, but I'm sure he'll hate the thought of the publicity. As for me, I'll probably lose my job at Queen Eleanor's.'

Phyllis leaned forward to pat her arm. 'Now, you're not to worry about it,' she said soothingly. 'The editor of the local paper is a very good friend of mine. When I first came to live here he came out in person to interview me for the paper, and we got along very well. He's a charming man. Just you leave it to me – I'll contact him first thing in the morning.'

Claire went to bed with mixed feelings that night. At least that was one problem solved. But as she switched off the light and lay listening to the sound of the sea she thought of Mike, lying in his bed at St Crispin's, worrying about being a burden to his family. Heaven only knew what interpretation he had put on his mother's news that she intended to marry again! In his present frame of mind he probably saw that as some kind of sacrifice too! As she closed her eyes and prepared for sleep her last thought was of the coming dinner party at which the fabled Sally was to be a guest. What effect would seeing her again have on Simon? Especially now that she was free again.

As luck would have it, the dinner party at Pilgrim's House coincided with her appearance in court. Apart from a brief flying visit to his mother Simon hadn't been over to Fritcham since their return from London, he had been too busy at St Winifred's, so she had had no chance to speak to him about the coming ordeal and had no way of knowing how he felt about it.

On the morning in question she woke with a feeling of impending doom. Phyllis, on the other hand, was cheerful. Today was the day she would be allowed to begin using what she called her 'new eye'.

Before leaving to drive into Kingsmere, Claire took the routine blood test and gave Phyllis her insulin injection, carefully filling in the chart. She bathed the eye, instilling the drops and replacing the dressing as usual. Trying to sound cheerful, she reminded Phyllis that this would probably be the last time. Sensing her tension, the older woman touched her hand.

'Don't worry, my dear,' she said. 'I've spoken to the editor of the *Recorder* on the telephone and he's promised me faithfully that no names will be reported. He told me in confidence that one of the other cases to be heard today is much more sensational and so will take priority over this one.'

Claire sighed. 'It isn't only that,' she said. 'It's the thought of my evidence putting someone behind bars that I hate.'

'But he did intend to commit a crime,' Phyllis reminded her. 'And I'm sure I don't have a point out to you that you might have been badly injured – or worse.'

Claire shuddered. 'I know – I'm very lucky. All the same, I'll be very glad when today is over.'

'Never mind. You'll have the dinner party to look forward to this evening,' Phyllis told her, smiling.

Claire tried to look happier. 'Yes – yes, of course,' she said. She hadn't needed reminding.

Her wait in the corridor outside the court room seemed endless. Simon was nowhere to be seen. At last she was called, and, stomach quaking, she went into the witness box. The accused looked younger than she remembered him; he looked both defiant and vulnerable at the same time. Claire averted her eyes.

She gave her evidence as clearly as she could, and when she came out into the corridor again she asked one of the ushers where she could get a cup of tea. Her mouth was dry and her head was aching dully. He directed her to a vending machine in an adjoining corridor.

'Better not leave the building yet, miss, just in case you're called again,' he told her.

She stared at him in dismay. 'Oh, is that likely?'

He smiled, shaking his head. 'Not very, but if you were needed it could hold things up.'

She found the drinks machine and inserted her money, swallowing the resultant hot coffee gratefully, her hands cupped around the comforting warmth of the plastic beaker. But she almost dropped it when a voice spoke softly behind her:

'Are you all right, Claire?'

She turned and found herself looking up into Simon's face. The sight of him was such a comfort that she felt her lip tremble. Without a word he took the half empty beaker from her, put it down on a nearby windowsill and pulled her into his arms, holding her close.

'Sorry I couldn't be here before, but it was difficult to get away.' He looked down at her, tipping her chin up so that he could look into her eyes. 'Was it ghastly?'

She bit her lip hard. 'I couldn't help

feeling sorry for him. Why do people do things like that? He must have been desperate.'

Simon shook his head. 'Don't waste your sympathy. He wouldn't have shown you any mercy if I hadn't come along when I did.'

'I'm sorry for involving you, Simon,' she said softly. 'I – I hope you don't mind, but I told your mother about it.'

'You told Phyllis? Dear God, did you *have* to?'

Claire's heart sank at the look on his face. 'I had to explain why I needed time off. But anyway, I'm glad I did. She knows the editor of the local paper and she spoke to him on our behalf. He's promised not to put either of our names in the paper.'

Simon held her away from him, a frown on his face. 'I wish you'd asked me first. I–'

A man appeared round the bend in the corridor. 'Excuse me, would you be Mr Simon Bonham?'

'That's right.'

'You're being called, sir.'

Simon dropped his hands to his sides. 'I'll have to go.'

'Simon, shall I see you later? I want to–' But he had disappeared round the corner before Claire had time to finish her sentence.

Hanging around outside the court, she learned a little later that the jury had retired. There would be no verdict until after lunch. She waited for Simon, but he did not appear, so she decided to go to the flat to get something to eat.

Letting herself in with her key, she found eggs and bacon in the fridge and made herself a hasty snack. She should have been hungry, she had eaten nothing at breakfast – but her stomach was in a worse turmoil now than it had been then.

She knew that her mother had lunch at the hospital canteen, so she decided to leave her a note, explaining briefly that she had been in town and stopped off to collect something to wear for the party that evening. Her heart sank when she remembered it – and the fact that she was once again in Simon's bad books. When he had taken her in his arms to comfort her this morning she had felt briefly that he really cared – then, as usual, she had done something to incur his displeasure again and spoilt everything. When would she *ever* get it right?

She finished her meal, then went through to her bedroom to find something suitable to wear this evening. Not that it mattered, she told herself glumly; Simon would hardly notice her once he set eyes on the fabulous Sally. That was one surprise meeting she would rather not have witnessed.

She chose a coral and white patterned dress in a softly flowing material, picking out a pair of white sandals to match. She was just packing them into a bag when the telephone rang. As she went through to the living room to answer it she wondered who could be ringing at this time of day. Everyone who knew them would realise that normally no one was here at this time of day. Expecting to find that the caller had the wrong number, she picked up the receiver.

'Hello – Kingsmere 8132.'

'Mrs Simms?'

'No, this is her daughter, Claire. Can I help? My mother is at work.'

'Ah, Miss Simms, this is St Crispin's School – Mr Cornish would like to speak to you.' There was a click, then the Head's voice came on the line.

'Good afternoon, Miss Simms. I thought I'd better contact you. I don't want to alarm you – and I can assure you that everything possible is being done–' Claire's mind raced ahead. Something had happened to Mike! An accident – he was badly hurt – worse! Panic gripped her as she asked shrilly:

'What's happened? Please tell me! Is it Mike?'

Mr Cornish's voice was cool. 'Please, don't be alarmed, Miss Simms, but I'm afraid he seems to have run away! It's all very distressing and no one here can think of any reason for it. He hasn't had any bad news from home lately, has he?'

CHAPTER THIRTEEN

Claire bit her lip. Surely her mother's impending marriage couldn't have upset Mike that much? It must be the thought of sitting for the Arnold Scholarship. She voiced the thought to the Headmaster. There was a pause, then he cleared his throat.

'It can't be that, Miss Simms. Michael has already taken the exam. His papers will have to go before the examination board, of course, but I can tell you – off the record, you understand – that his chances of gaining a place are excellent. In fact, since Speech Day the boy has seemed more settled.'

Claire sighed. There could be only one reason for Mike's running away, if what Mr Cornish said was true. Misinterpreting her silence, the Headmaster said hurriedly:

'Please try not to be unduly alarmed, Miss Simms. I can't think he can have gone far, and I assure you that everything possible is being done. The police have been informed and there are people from the school out looking for him. I felt it was my duty to inform you – and of course to ask you to let me know should he turn up at home.'

'Of course – thank you. Is there anything at all I can do?'

'Not really. I shall contact you again as soon as there's any news.'

Claire's mind was working fast. Her mother would probably have already left for her weekend with her prospective sister-in-law – and she herself would not be here at the flat for much longer. Quickly she explained the situation to Mr Cornish, gave him Phyllis Lattimer's telephone number, thanked him again and rang off.

She made herself a strong cup of coffee and sat down to work out what to do, forcing herself to think calmly. Ringing Queen Eleanor's to check, she confirmed her suspicion that Dr Phillips and her mother had already left for their weekend. There was no way she could get in touch with them, so she would have to do what she could herself. She wrote a note, addressed it to Mike and pinned it to the front door. If he did turn up here at least he would know where to find her. She had a sudden worrying vision of her mother arriving at St

Crispin's on Sunday afternoon only to be told that Mike was missing, but dismissed it quickly. He would be found by then. He *had* to be!

She arrived back at the court in time to hear the jury's verdict of Guilty. The youth was sentenced to a spell in a detention centre. Claire hoped that it would do him some good; surely it had to be better than prison? At least her part in it was done. Simon was not there, and in a way she was glad. She might have been tempted to tell him about Mike, and she was determined to keep this problem to herself.

At Pilgrim's House the preparations for the dinner party were well under way, and Claire threw herself into helping with them, trying to put all thoughts of what was happening to Mike from her mind. There was nothing she could do, she kept telling herself. It was out of her hands now. The police and the staff at St Crispin's had the situation under control and would contact her the moment there was any news.

Professor Darnley arrived alone soon after six o'clock to examine Phyllis's eye. In a darkened room he removed the dressing and inspected it thoroughly with an ophthalmoscope, eventually pronouncing its satisfactory progress.

'You can leave the dressing off now, though I daresay you'll find the light rather uncomfortable at first,' he warned. 'Wear your dark glasses until you feel you can do without them – and in bright sunlight, of course. When you've had a rest we shall have to think about tackling the other one for you, though there's plenty of time before you need think about that.'

Claire, who had been standing by in case she was needed, fetched Phyllis's dark glasses and put them on for her. The older woman was elated.

'It's wonderful – a miracle!' she enthused. 'You must come and have a drink at once to celebrate.' She slipped an arm through Claire's. 'You too, my dear.' She turned to the Professor. 'I don't know what I would have done without this dear girl over the past weeks.'

'I've done very little,' Claire protested. 'You're so independent.'

But Phyllis shook her head. 'You've been a tower of strength – you'll never know. It means such a lot to have someone who really *cares!*'

Claire had been wondering where the Professor's daughter was, but over a relaxed drink he cleared up the mystery. She would be coming along later in a taxi, he told them.

'She had some notes to type up for me back at the hotel,' he explained with a smile. 'And of course, she wanted to have time to do all the things you ladies feel so vital before you can go out to dinner – hair, make-up and so on. Knowing Sally, I'm sure the effect will be worth it.'

Privately, Claire thought so too. Excusing herself, she left the two together while she went upstairs to change. When she came down Simon had arrived. He was standing by the drawing room window with a drink in his hand. Claire had never seen him in a dinner jacket before, and he looked so handsome that her heart twisted painfully as he turned to face her. His eyes raked her from head to toe, taking in her appearance coolly as Phyllis remarked:

'How charming you look, my dear. Simon, pour her a sherry. We're still waiting for our other guest. As soon as she arrives we can go in to dinner.'

As Simon went to pour the drink, Phyllis shook her head behind his back, holding a finger to her lips to indicate that he was still in the dark as to the identity of the missing guest.

He walked over to Claire, handing her the glass of sherry. 'What was the outcome this afternoon?' he asked quietly. 'I take it you went back after lunch?'

She nodded. 'The verdict was Guilty. He's to be sent to a detention centre.'

'Let's hope he learns his lesson.' Simon looked at her. 'Are you feeling better now it's over? You're still rather pale.'

'I'm fine, thanks.' So much for Phyllis's remark about her appearance. Simon certainly didn't seem to share it! After all the trouble she had taken with her make-up, all he could say was that she 'looked pale'!

The doorbell rang, and Claire's ears strained for the sound of voices in the hall. Simon was still speaking, but she was unaware of what he was saying as the door opened and Mrs Winters ushered Phyllis's final guest in. Sally stood in the doorway – making the perfect entrance. Had she delayed her arrival on purpose? Claire asked herself wryly. She wore a clinging black dress that managed to reveal her perfect figure while still covering most of it up. She wore her vibrant auburn hair in an upswept style, with curling tendrils caressing the creamy skin of her neck and forehead. Phyllis went towards her, hands outstretched.

'Sally, my dear, how lovely to see you again after all these years!'

Claire hardly dared to look at Simon, but when she did steal a glance at him she was surprised to see that he didn't seem at all amazed by his mother's guest. Phyllis turned to him with a smile.

'Simon, I've been keeping Sally as a surprise for you. You didn't expect to see *her* this evening, did you?'

Sally laughed. 'I'm sorry to steal your thunder, Phyllis, but Simon and I had tea together only this afternoon. We met at St Winifred's where Father was lecturing.' She turned the full force of her dazzling smile on Simon, crossing the room to stand next to him. 'He took me to his delightful new home and we talked for simply ages, catching up with all the news, didn't we, darling?' She slipped an arm intimately through his. 'He's matured so handsomely. When we ran into each other in the corridor this afternoon he was wearing these *distinguished* glasses. He quite swept me off my feet!'

Afterwards, Claire remembered very little about the meal, except that Sally had monopolised the conversation. She kept everyone enthralled with her stories of her life in America and of all the exotic places she had travelled with her businessman husband. She was scintillating, witty and clever as well as being beautiful, and made Claire feel dull and tongue-tied by comparison. Any man would be flattered to have the attention of such a glamorous creature, so how must Simon, who was once very much in love with her, be feeling?

Her thoughts turned unhappily to Mike, wondering where he was. She imagined him cold and hungry – huddled in a field maybe, or in the corner of some barn for warmth. Could he have arrived at the flat only to find no one there? She tried hard to swallow the lump that rose in her throat. Although Mrs Winters' dinner was delicious, eating was an ordeal.

After dinner Phyllis played the piano for her guests and for a little while Claire was soothed by the music. Then Sally rose and announced that she must leave.

'I've had such a wonderful evening. Thank you, Phyllis.' She bent to kiss her hostess on the cheek. 'Don't feel you have to come too, Father,' she said. 'I don't want to spoil your evening, but I still have some notes to type for tomorrow's lecture. I'm sure Simon will take me back to Kingsmere, won't you, darling?' She smiled at him in what Claire thought was a very meaningful way, and he responded at once.

'Of course.' He downed the last of his brandy and stood up, turning to his mother.

'I'll say good night too. And thank you for a wonderful dinner.' He glanced briefly at Claire. 'Good night.' For a moment their eyes met and she tried to read what was in them. It wasn't possible. Their blue depths told her nothing – unlike Sally's, which were full of anticipation and promise as she smiled up at him, slipping her hand invitingly into his.

Claire listened to the sound of Simon's car as it receded into the night. Phyllis got out her backgammon board and invited Professor Darnley to play.

'I had hoped we might have had a hand of bridge,' she said, 'but there seems little hope of that now.' She looked doubtfully at Claire. 'Are you quite happy, dear?'

Claire rose, feigning a yawn. 'If you'll excuse me, I think I'll go to bed,' she said.

Phyllis looked sympathetic. 'Of course, I'd forgotten – you've had a traumatic day, haven't you? And I haven't even asked you about it.' She squeezed Claire's hand. 'We'll have a long talk tomorrow. Good night, dear.'

In her room Claire opened the window and stared out into the darkness, leaning her elbows on the sill. The sound of the sea was strangely hypnotic and comforting, and she listened for a while to the thud and roar of the waves on the shore and the rattle of the shingle. She wondered if Simon had really taken Sally back to her hotel or if her leaving early was something they had arranged in advance. She was so sophisticated and confident; if she decided that she wanted Simon back she would know just how to snare him. Too restless to undress, Claire lay down on the bed, her mind swirling with thoughts. Were they at Simon's snug little house? She tortured herself, imagining them together, sharing intimate moments – rekindling old fires, even planning a future life together. She closed her eyes, turning her head on the pillow to try to blot out the images. But somehow it only served to create new ones – Mike, alone and afraid, feeling shut out. Wanting to go back but not knowing how to without losing face. If she could only find him – talk to him!

At last she decided to ring the school. It was late, but she couldn't go to sleep without knowing if he had been found. She told herself that they would have rung her had there been any news, but nevertheless she got up and went quietly downstairs. The Professor's car was still in the drive and she could hear quiet voices coming from the drawing room. There was a telephone in the kitchen and Mrs Winters had gone home hours ago. No one would hear if she rang from there.

With trembling fingers she dialled the number, listening to the ringing at the other end with rising apprehension. At last there was a click as the receiver was lifted.

'Hello – St Crispin's School. Headmaster speaking.'

'Oh, thank goodness! It's Claire Simms, Mr Cornish. I'm sorry to ring so late, but I wondered if there was any news about my brother?'

'I'm afraid we haven't found him yet, Miss Simms. I've been hoping all evening that we might get a call from you. We've discovered something that could be useful, however: it seems that Michael borrowed money from another boy. He's in possession of enough to buy a rail ticket home. I do feel that at least he won't come to too much harm as long as he has some cash.'

Claire's spirits rose – only to sink again. If Mike hadn't come home, where *had* he gone? Anything might have happened. He was very trusting – if he had confided in someone that he had money–

'I – I think I'd better go over to the flat to see if he's turned up there,' she said. 'If I find him I'll ring you back at once.'

A sudden sound made her spin round. The kitchen door was open and Simon stood framed in the doorway, looking at her with concern. They stared at each other, while Mr Cornish's voice continued unheard at the other end of the line. Slowly, Claire replaced the receiver.

'All evening I knew something was wrong. I had to come back and find out what it was. Want to tell me about it?' Simon closed the door and crossed the kitchen towards her. When she didn't answer he took her by the shoulders and turned her, forcing her to look at him.

'Claire! What is it?' he demanded. 'Who's missing?'

'It's Mike,' she whispered. 'It seems he's run away from school. I expect he's all right. It's just – just – not knowing–' She had tried very hard to sound calm, to give the impression that she wasn't too worried, but it was no use. However hard she swallowed she couldn't stop the tears from welling up and overflowing. 'My mother is away for the weekend. She's planning to marry Dr Phillips, you see, and they've gone to stay with his sister. She telephoned Mike to tell him and I'm afraid he was upset.'

Simon frowned, holding her away from him to look into her eyes.

'Your mother gave him news like that when he was already unsettled at school?'

She shook her head. 'I hadn't told her about that! She didn't know!'

He shook his head. 'Oh, Claire – *Claire!* Why do you try to take it all on your own shoulders? You silly girl! Now perhaps you can see the folly of it!' He pulled her close, letting her cry on his shoulder for a few moments before he asked: 'Where were you planning to go when I came in?'

'To the flat – to see if he was there. I left a note for him. I couldn't think what else to do.'

Simon shook her gently. 'Why didn't you tell someone – me – my mother?'

'I couldn't. Not this evening, with the dinner party and everything. Anyway, who cares about my problems?'

'*I* do, you idiot girl!' He turned her towards the door and gave her a gentle push. 'Get a coat while I slip in and tell Phyllis what's happening. You're in no state to go by yourself.'

They were both silent on their way to Kingsmere, each busy with their own thoughts. As he drew up outside the flat Simon turned to her.

'Now look, if he isn't there it doesn't necessarily mean anything.'

Claire looked at him, her eyes huge grey pools of fear. 'No – no, I know,' she whispered.

He reached out and drew her close. 'Don't look like that, sweetheart. I know how you feel, believe me, I do. I thought I'd never feel close to anyone in that way until–' he broke off, looking down at her. 'Come on, let's go and look for him, shall we?'

Mike wasn't at the flat. The note Claire had left was gone, though. It looked as though he had been there.

'Your mother's address was in it,' said Claire, her hopes rising. 'He must be trying to get to me there.'

'Right, come on!' Simon took her hand and hurried her down the stairs again. Back in the car she looked at him.

'What about your evening? Shouldn't you be with Sally?'

He took his eyes off the road to stare at

her. 'I took her back to her hotel, that was all.'

She said nothing, knowing that Sally had certainly intended far more than that. How disappointed she must have been! She tried hard to quell the feeling of joy that surged into her heart. 'Had you heard about my mother's engagement to Dr Phillips?' she asked, changing the subject.

'You must be joking!' laughed Simon. 'The grapevine at Queen Eleanor's has been positively twanging with it!' He looked at her. 'Are you happy about it?'

She nodded. 'Certainly, but even if I weren't, it's her life, isn't it?'

'Does that mean that you'll be able to get on with yours now?' he asked.

She looked surprised. 'I don't know what you mean.'

'I mean will you now be able to think about your own future – plan for yourself without having to wonder how it fits in with everyone else's life?' He laughed at her bemused face. 'I really don't think you'd know where to start, would you?'

At Pilgrim's House the Professor's car had gone, but as they stood in the hall, taking off their coats, they could hear voices coming, from the drawing room. Simon opened the door to reveal two people seated one on either side of a table drawn up to the fire-place. They were deeply engrossed in a game of backgammon. Beside them on another small table was a large mug of steaming cocoa and a plate of sandwiches. Phyllis looked up.

'Ah, there you are at last! This young brother of yours has been beating me hollow, Claire. By rights he should have been in bed hours ago, but I knew you'd want to see him, so I let him stay up until you got back.' She got up from the table. 'It's all right – I took the liberty of ringing the Headmaster, so the heat's off.' She took Simon's arm. 'I daresay there are family matters to be discussed. Come along, Simon, your cocoa is in the kitchen. I must say I'm enjoying myself – I've always wanted to make cocoa for a runaway boy!'

They set off for St Crispin's the following morning after an early breakfast, Mike sitting in the front of the Alfa Romeo with Simon. The two got along well and this morning, after a long talk, Mike seemed reassured and happy to return to school, looking forward to his mother's visit on the following day and meeting his prospective stepfather. Simon stood them both a slap-up lunch at The Haycock before Mike was safely handed over to his housemaster.

Claire went to see Mr Cornish, explaining as best she could the changing situation at home and how Mike was happier now that he was in full possession of all the facts.

As she got back into the car beside Simon she heaved a sigh of relief. He turned to her.

'So – where now?'

She shrugged. 'Back to Fritcham, I suppose.'

He looked at her for a long minute. 'Your life seems fraught with dramas lately, doesn't it? I think you deserve a little time off.'

'Oh, but your mother–?' she began, but he put a finger against her lips.

'Just for once will you stop thinking about other people?'

'She *is* my employer,' she reminded him.

'And she was the first to make the suggestion. In fact I had strict instructions not to bring you home until midnight at the very earliest.'

Claire looked down at her hands. 'Oh. I see– It was her idea.'

Very gently Simon lifted her chin until his eyes looked gravely into hers. 'Claire, there's a lot I want to say to you. I think–' He stopped as a car drew up next to theirs in the car park and a noisy family spilled excitedly out of it. 'Let's get away from here,' he said, turning from her to start the engine. 'Somewhere quiet where we can talk.'

They found a secluded spot in a lane off the motorway and got out of the car to walk through the peat-scented pinewoods. Claire found herself suddenly shy as they walked, racking her brain for something to say to break the silence, but when she spoke Simon began to say something too. They broke off, laughing, and Simon caught her hand and drew her to him.

'Claire, now that I've got you here alone I don't know how to begin,' he said, his eyes searching hers. 'You'll never know how much you've changed my life – my whole way of thinking.'

She stared at him in amazement. '*I* have?'

'Yes.' He lifted a hand to touch her cheek. 'For years I've considered myself free – independent, self-sufficient. I thought I didn't need anyone. When we first met I was attracted to you – much more strongly that I wanted to be. For a while I fought it, then I thought maybe I should stop fighting and get you out of my system.' He smiled wryly. 'I didn't bargain for your sweetness, the things you'd teach me about living and relationships.'

Claire shook her head, not recognising herself at all. 'I haven't the slightest idea what you mean.'

He pulled her to him, laughing gently. 'I believe you. That's part of your charm. I told myself that if I hadn't kissed you, hadn't held you in my arms, I'd have been able to shake off the feeling, but deep down I know it's not true. Each time I've watched you getting yourself into a mess, all for someone else's sake, I've had this maddening – irresistible urge to rush in and rescue you. Phyllis crystallised it for me last night. She said you'd "humanised" me!'

Claire frowned. 'Phyllis knows? But she invited Sally to dinner last night. I was under the impression that she hoped you and she–'

'She was laying a ghost,' Simon interrupted. 'Or so she thought. I got over Sally years ago. I only kept her photograph as a reminder. When I met her again the other day, listened to her empty chatter, her materialistic views, I knew I'd had a lucky escape.'

His hand cupped her chin, raising her face to his, and when their lips met Claire felt happiness surge up within her. His kiss had everything – tenderness, passion, longing. It told Claire all the things she had ever dreamed of being told, and she clung to him, wanting the enchantment of the moment to go on for ever, trying to put into her response all the things she found too deep to trust to words.

They walked on, arms about each other, to the top of a ridge, where they could see the rolling woods and the sea beyond. Claire looked up at Simon.

'Phyllis is fine now. She doesn't really need me any longer. I don't think she ever did really, did she?'

He smiled. 'Maybe you've guessed that I was the one who needed you most. When I suggested you took the job, I was being selfish as usual.' He pulled her close to his side. 'As the new ophthalmic unit won't be ready for at least another month it rather looks as though you'll be out of a job, doesn't it?' He looked down at her ruefully.

She shrugged. 'Perhaps I could find another temporary patient.'

He took her shoulders, turning her to him, his eyes twinkling. 'Don't you dare. You're booked as from this moment, Nurse Simms!' When she shook her head he laughed. 'I'm asking you to marry me! If we hurry we'll just have time for a honeymoon!' The smile left his face and he looked into her eyes gravely. 'Perhaps I'm taking too much for granted. Perhaps I'm just another of your worthy causes.'

She smiled up at him, gently teasing. 'Or could it be that you've forgotten to tell me something?'

He drew her close, wrapping his arms around her and burying his face in her hair. 'I love you,' he whispered softly. 'I need practice at saying things like that, but I'm sure I'll soon become an expert with you as my teacher.' He raised his head to look down at her. 'And now do I qualify for an answer?'

Claire couldn't find even the one word needed. Her heart was too full of happiness, but she drew his head down to hers to kiss him, leaving him in no doubt – no doubt at all.

The publishers hope that this book has given you enjoyable reading. Large Print Books are especially designed to be as easy to see and hold as possible. If you wish a complete list of our books please ask at your local library or write directly to:

Dales Large Print Books
Magna House, Long Preston,
Skipton, North Yorkshire.
BD23 4ND

This Large Print Book, for people
who cannot read normal print,
is published under the auspices of

THE ULVERSCROFT FOUNDATION